SOLDIER BLUE

SOLDIER BLUE

T. V. Olsen

There were only two survivors of the massacre. CRESTA LEE, saucy New York girl come west to be an officer's lady, and recently escaped from two years' captivity with the Cheyenne. HONUS GANT, bumbling farmer-school teacher turned soldier.

They disliked each other on sight.

But they had to team up in order to survive – especially when the Cheyenne chief came looking for the white woman who had been his wife for two years.

Also by T. V. Olsen *The Stalking Moon*
Bitter Grass

Soldier Blue

T. V. OLSEN

SPHERE BOOKS LIMITED
30/32 Gray's Inn Road, London WC1X 8JL

First published in Great Britain in 1971
by Sphere Books Ltd.
Orginal title: *Arrow in the Sun*
© T. V. Olsen 1969
Reprinted May 1971

Set in Linotype Times Roman

Printed in Great Britain by
Hazell Watson & Viney Ltd,
Aylesbury, Bucks

SOLDIER BLUE

Chapter One

Captain Battles was worried. A soft man in his forties with brittle almond eyes in a face that resembled a pink prune, he was richly endowed with the gopherish nerves and uneasy digestion that was the lot of most Army paymasters. And the captain, more fretful than most, had chafed unhappily since the transfer from his comfortable swivel chair in the recruiting headquarters at Jefferson Barracks to the rough transverse seat of a cavalry paywagon.

His wagon was a Dougherty—ambulance, the Army called it —and the canvas curtains which covered sides and rear had been rolled up to give Captain Battles, in the vehicle's stern, a grand view of the surrounding country.

Not that there was much to see. To the right, tawny rolling slopes of buffalo grass broken by sandstone outcrops. To the left, the Janroe River, mostly a sallow east-west trickle with a deep prowling back-eddy here and there.

The old military road that ran in a rough crow's-flight between the Pine Hills Agency and Fort Reunion made a slight detour here to follow the angled slash of river bed in a north-easterly way. The stream's emerald border of scrub willow and a few cottonwoods offered a modest relief from the grinding monotony of yellow-grassed plains. Inauspicious cheer.

Anyway Captain Battles was not interested in scenery. Nor in the attractive young woman who shared his wagon, sitting on the rear-facing front seat just behind the driver's awninged perch. He was, as always, a little ill from the motion of the wagon and irritable with the increasing heat of midday. And worried.

Private Honus Gant, one of the first two troopers heading up the double column riding six yards behind the Dougherty, watched the captain's head swivel right to left on his plump fiery neck as he sweatily conned the landscape. And albeit Private Gant had taken a warm dislike to the captain, he was not altogether out of sympathy.

Practically speaking, of course, there was nothing to worry about these days. Almost nothing.

Some time ago the tribes of the southern plains, Comanche and Kiowa and Southern Cheyenne, had been rounded up and placed on reservation. As recently as a year ago, the northern plains tribes, the Sioux of Red Cloud, Sitting Bull, Crazy Horse, and remnants of the Northern Cheyenne led by Dull Knife and Two Moons, had continued stubbornly to resist.

But Red Cloud had come onto reservation, bringing thousands of his followers with him. The military's fierce harassment of the remaining Sioux and Cheyenne after the crushing humiliation of the Little Big Horn had reduced them to broken, scattered bands. Dull Knife and his people, who had once held sway across this heartland of all the plains country between the Missouri and the Rockies, had been sent away from their Powder River hunting grounds, down to Fort Reno and the Darlington Agency. . . .

Still Private Honus Gant, like the captain, felt the skin gooseflesh uneasily between his shoulder blades.

A bad place, this. Just beyond the Janroe's serpentine sparkle lifted a rim of drab easy hills that formed the north flank of the river valley. Too easy for the sun-drugged brain to conjure up fantasies of a line of painted warriors waiting just beyond that concealing summit. And the twin-columned guard detail —the paymaster's escort for the hundred-odd miles separating

Fort Kearsage and Fort Reunion—made a tempting target. The troop could be caught in the open and cut to pieces from those mild-looking hills. . . .

The paywagon was positioned in the middle of the detail. Up at the head of the column now, First Lieutenant Rufus Spingarn spoke briefly to Sergeant O'Hearn, then swung his bay around and rode back to the Dougherty.

Again he wheeled the animal and rode apace of the front wheel, gallantly sweeping off his hat. "How are you, Miss Lee? Holding up, I trust?"

With the Dougherty's flat roof nicely shading the passengers, Miss Cresta Lee had removed her wide-brimmed straw hat for coolness. Wind lightly toiled with the richly dark brown mass of her hair which she wore brushed out, a blue ribbon its sole confinement. Ill-fitting as was her faded brown cambric dress (a castoff that had belonged to the agent's wife) her figure proclaimed its burgeoning youth—and would have done so in sackcloth.

Not over five feet tall, she struck you as neither short nor small. Ripely compact rather: like a traditional milkmaid. The plains sun and wind that should have dried and darkened her skin to the color and texture of old saddle leather (lot of most white frontier women, not to say of a girl who had spent two years as a Cheyenne captive) had warmed her skin to a glow of living gold.

"It beats out riding a travois pony all day, I'd say, Lieutenant." Her voice was bell-clear, half amused, half indifferent, holding Lieutenant Spingarn neatly at arm's length.

"Ha ha, yes, well, I guess it would," said Spingarn, and dropped back beside Captain Battles' seat.

"Well, sir," he said with impudent good cheer, "halfway to Reunion and not a bloody red devil sighted. Not even a blanket Injun with a plowhorse."

Captain Battles eyed his subordinate with an ill-concealed distaste. Everything about the thirty-three-year-old lieutenant was calculated to set the captain's precise nature on edge.

Once more, Honus Gant could sympathize. It wasn't enough

that Lieutenant Spingarn was an inconscionably handsome lout: he affected every detail in dress of his idol, the late Boy General. Soft-tanned kneeboots, red silk neckerchief, fringed cowboy gauntlets—and of course a flowing Custer mustache. His broad black Stetson was folded rakishly up at the sides Custer-style and pinned up in front with an enlisted man's crossed-saber insignia.

What was particularly unnerving to a man of the captain's digestion was that First Lieutenant Spingarn affected not only the dress but the finely careless airs of his idol. And the fiasco of Little Big Horn was just a year old: still a freshly memorable wound in the nation's pride.

Battles swept his hand out in an irritable semicircle. "Wouldn't you say, Mr. Spingarn, that this is a likely place to put out flankers?"

"Well," Spingarn said with mock gravity, "if that's an *order*, sir—"

Which remark was playing dirty billiards, in a way. Battles was observing ordinary etiquette by not pulling rank and ordering the younger officer to take a simple precaution. As paymaster for forts and base camps throughout the Department of the Platte, it was the sole concern of Captain Battles to see that the payroll was delivered punctually. He enjoyed the amount of esteem that any natural-born desk soldier did if he discharged his duties with a modicum of competence.

Spingarn was in command of the guard escort. Moreover he was, for all his dash, silk and fringes, an Indian fighter. He had been with Crook on the Rosebud; he had played a hand in MacKenzie's slaughter of Dull Knife's village last year.

Honus watched Battles' profile turn turkey-wattle red. He tried to salvage an advantage by massive sarcasm: "Naturally, Mister, I wouldn't presume to advise *you*. Arch-foe of the redman. Brevetted a colonel after Cemetery Ridge—"

"At nineteen, yessir!" Spingarn barked. "Thank you!"

The captain held onto himself by sheer will. He even grinned, his face like an amiable deathmask of rosy wet putty. "Heh heh, look here now, Spingarn"—mingling a half-deferent informality with a benign patience—"even a green old duffer like me can see we're as wide open as fish in a barrel."

Spingarn cocked a highly sardonic brow. "Yes indeed, sir. On the other hand, nobody's ever heard of a gang of road agents large enough to dare attack a well-armed escort of this size."

"Very good," Battles said fretfully. "I wasn't thinking of your run-of-the-mill Western desperadoes. The Indians—"

"Ah yes, Indians. What do you say we consult a *real* authority, Captain?" Spingarn turned his head and called, "*Sergeant!*"

Sergeant O'Hearn, Troop N's top—and a top noncom in any man's troop—cantered his mount back to the Dougherty and threw a salute. He was a great swarthy lath of a man with uneasy eyes and a long-jawed face that twitched with yeasty grimaces.

"Yessir?"

"Sergeant, have you ever heard of a paymaster's detail being attacked by Indians?"

"No, Lieutenant. Never been such a thing. The reddies ain't caring about money, gold or paper." O'Hearn harrumphed unhappily and gave Captain Battles an apologetic look. "They ain't known to attack soldiers unless the soldiers is out after hostiles. Then the beggars is most likely to decoy 'em into an ambush. *Tac*-tically, o' course"—O'Hearn's face was twitching incredibly in his agonized determination to straddle fence with opposed superiors—"this here's a road to have a care on. T'was up till a year ago, anyways. But all the Shy-Annies is rounded up and gone to Darlington."

Captain Battles glared fussily and mopped his face with a silk handkerchief. "I see. And what about Spotted Wolf? Didn't he break with Dull Knife? Isn't he still active in this region? Or is Spotted Wolf just an official mirage?" Battles was very sarcastic: he looked suddenly at the girl. "I believe you'd agree he's real, wouldn't you, Miss Lee?"

It was the first time he had spoken directly to the girl who had ridden in his paywagon since yesterday. It was also (knowing what they all did) a remark of cutting brutality.

Miss Lee did not turn a hair. "I certainly would." Her tone was calm, normal, agreeable. She might have been answering a comment on the weather.

"Uh-huh," Spingarn parried blandly, "but even Spotted Wolf has never attacked a paymaster. However, I expect you'll feel easier in your belly, sir, if I mount a couple of flank guards. Ser-*geant!*"

"Yes, sir. Right away."

O'Hearn loped down the column, bawling out names of four troopers. These grumblingly fell out. O'Hearn dispatched two of them across the buff slopes to the south. The other two rode through the river shallows and, splitting apart then, cut out of sight to the north.

Captain Battles slumped back on his seat, morose but pudgily relieved. Spingarn rode up by the girl again, lounging gracefully in his saddle and ignoring Battles as he carried on a quiet run of one-sided chatter with her.

The heat was gusty and soporific, rising off the rolls of land in shimmering veils. Luckily Honus never had to dwell long on the depressing, infinite sameness of the country. As a U.S. cavalryman, he had a foolproof diversion: he was God's own monument to soldierly martyrdom.

He could remove the suffocating hotbox that was the natty cavalry blouse of dark blue wool (no summer issue), but he still had to endure an itching torment of heavy shirt of gray flannel, worn next to his skin (because the Army did not issue undershirts). The sun broiled; he merely simmered. The resultant sweat nicely abetted a prickly rash that abetted the raw sore being chafed into the flesh of his right shoulder by the steady gouging friction of his gunsling (because the Army did not issue saddle boots either). The three-inch-wide black leather strap supported the carrying ring of his heavy Springfield, whose muzzle rested dutifully in a round socket lashed to the saddle. That saddle, of course, was George B. McClellan's peculiar contribution to the horse army's supreme misery. You could stop right there, because after a day in a McClellan, the seat of your agony precluded undue preoccupation with other concerns. The world could end and you wouldn't care.

Honus Gant enjoyed several extra degrees of torment because of his lank and bony frame. He had six feet of height, but its most salient features ran to hands and feet and joints. His hands had the splayed, big-knuckled look of any farm lad's; they were plentifully freckled, as was his thin and amazingly boyish face.

Here, though, the freckles were almost lost in the ruddy brown that had finally succeeded the repeated peeling sunburns to which the blasting plains sun had treated his fair skin. It was, withal, a pleasant unhandsome face, at twenty-five almost beardless, topped with hair like a brush fire. When left to grow, it spilled in flaming fantails over his brow and ears and neck. Closely cropped now, it still blazed with sly exuberance under the floppy, raw-edged brim of his black Jeff Davis hat.

Too many years in a classroom, away from the good solid grind of farm toil, had softened him, Honus had found to his chagrin. But N Troop's O'Hearn had seen diligently to a collection of blisters and sore limbs that quickly put back calluses on Honus' palms, solid ropes of muscle on his shoulders. Unluckily the recent weeks had also pared off what little padding his lean buttocks had boasted.

His pale blue eyes that had been rather dyspeptic and lackluster were now alert, watchful, almost a plainsman's eyes. And unhappy.

To round out a multitude of miseries, there was Private Menzies jogging alongside him. Private Menzies' bonus to the pleasant morning of Honus Gant was a generous belching and flatulence that celebrated the usual beans breakfast.

He hacked raucously, spewing a noxious geyser of tobacco juice at the cloud of flies. "Jesus," he muttered. "To think she's been *had* by an Injun. You picture that?"

"No," Honus said. "I'm assuming you have enough pictures for both of us."

Menzies placidly rolled his plug cud in a whiskered jaw. "So's

15

the lootenant, boy. So's he. Got a right smart more'n looking on his mind, too."

Menzies was very dependable that way, having all the tact and sensitivity of a bull bison. The worst of it was that he had a kind of gravelly hog-ignorant likableness that Honus would have found intolerable in a civilian companion. The Army bred buddies from strange breeds.

Menzies had taken to Honus from the first, not put off by the latter's early aloofness. Grudging acceptance came first, then friendship. Buddies. To get drunk with, loan your last dime to, or get battered three ways from Sunday with in a saloon brawl.

Not that Honus drank very much. He had a reason for saving his pay. Besides, whiskey usually made him sick, which he supposed was a good thing. At the same time, a capacity for liquor would have let him spice a soldier's lot with something besides privation and boredom.

As it was, he would settle for just getting out of this man's Army directly his first enlistment was up. Which would be in exactly six months and thirteen days. . . .

Meantime he let anything that was convenient engage his bitter fancy. Up ahead, Miss Cresta Lee was nodding absently to Lieutenant Spingarn's low, persuasive voice.

Menzies, with the brutal directness of any simple rutting male, had driven the nail through the board. Lieutenant Spingarn's intentions were transparent, even if one didn't know that he was engaged to the daughter of Colonel Wilson back at Kearsage. The detail would be several days and nights on the trail: idle evening hours must be filled. Nights had been romantically warm of late, clear and starlit. Facts that would have received due consideration in Mr. Spingarn's calculations. . . .

By now every man on the detail knew Cresta Lee's story. How she had come out from Boston two years ago to marry a young lieutenant stationed at Fort Reunion. Perhaps twenty miles from her destination, the stagecoach had been attacked by Cheyennes. Bodies of driver, guard, passengers were left pin-cushioned with arrows—all the passengers but one.

Three weeks ago she had staggered into the Pine Hills Agency, thin and exhausted, wearing the camp garb of a Cheyenne woman. She had made an escape on foot from Spotted Wolf's band.

Directly he had her story, Agent Terry Long had telegraphed Fort Reunion, informing Lieutenant John McNair that his fiancée was alive and well. Lieutenant McNair had just as promptly wired back urging Cresta Lee to journey at once to Reunion and join him in matrimony as originally planned. ("Just as if," the gossipy Mrs. Long had told Honus and some other interested troopers, "*nothing* had even *happened* in those two years. Which of course *couldn't* be the case." Trace of pecky acid in the words before a maternal mist had softened her eyes. "Ah well, poor child. She's suffered enough, and it's not ended. But she's lucky in her young lieutenant. I vow, this McNair must be a saint among men!")

But eighty miles of empty country lay between the agency and Fort Reunion. McNair could not break away from his duties to come for her; Agent Long was occupied with his own affairs. Travelers between fort and agency were far between, those few shifty and untrustworthy. Not till yesterday, with the arrival of the paymaster's wagon from Fort Kearsage, had Miss Lee found her escort to Reunion and her lieutenant.

Made wroth though he was by her very existence, Captain Battles had been unable gracefully to refuse the favor. He did pointedly ignore her, which seemed to eminently suit Miss Lee.

Her face was clear, indifferent, utterly serene. Or smug? Perhaps she had a right to smugness: her lieutenant was taking her back without a pause, and she could afford to ignore the Battleses of the world. (Still you wondered: Indians had been known merely to enslave white women, working them hard and letting the squaws abuse them, not harming them otherwise.)

Even if you were Honus Gant, and inclined to be a bit puritan in thought, word and deed, you had to hand it to this girl for keeping her head up. Yet Honus was bothered. There was something vaguely *indecent* about her very indifference, as if she were beyond all shame or regret.

Just as (in a way) it was an affront to decency that anyone should survive her experience bursting with health and vigor (and be unpardonably pretty into the bargain). Mrs. Long had said Cresta Lee had been more dead than alive when she reached their post. Maybe, but she could hardly have been emaciated, for after just a couple of weeks of rest and good food, she was far from skinny.

Suddenly her full gaze turned on Honus. Her eyes were intense as agates, sending a shock through him. He realized how intently he had been staring. He dropped his glance, feeling the blood gushing to his face.

Good God, was he starting to share Menzies' brute fantasies? He denied it. But he shouldn't have stared.

He couldn't interpret the look in her face—so wise and so cool. But Honus was sure of one thing. If Cresta Lee was remarkably free of bitterness, she was just as unhampered by what an increasingly cynical age still called Innocence. . . .

The curving river valley had sloped gradually toward higher land, almost vanishing while the stream's cutbanks grew steep, tall. It was easier to spell out the surrounding terrain.

The troopers rode with eyes half-shuttered against the glare. The columns were paired ant-files crawling across the face of eternal, empty stillness. Sounds? A softness of wind curling down young grass in the bottoms, a sullen buzz of flies, creak of Dougherty axles, dry brittle blades of high-hill grass flaking to powder under the thud of hoofs. . . .

The attack came with shattering suddenness.

One moment you were drowsing along with the slumping column, sore and sleepy. Next moment a savage volley of whoops.

The two flank guards who had gone north came racing into view across a rise as if the devil were at their heels. A loose knot of mounted warriors poured across the skyline behind them.

Rifles cracked. Both troopers went spilling from their saddles. And then the Indians were rushing down the hillside toward the column at full gallop, screaming war shouts, firing.

Chapter Two

It was Sergeant O'Hearn whose commands rapped the stunned troopers into action. Both Spingarn and Battles were slow to respond, and then they followed O'Hearn's order. The sergeant was yelling for the men to take shelter in a close-woven maze of thickets that sprawled some two hundred feet to their right.

Nobody needed a second urging. The whole troop broke for the brush motte in a disordered rout.

In the kaleidoscopic bedlam of these first minutes, Honus was aware of many things at once. But the impressions were imperfect, fragmentary. A wounded horse screaming, rearing, going down in a kicking heap, pinning his rider. The Dougherty wagon bouncing across the hummocky ground, the driver hoorawing his team furiously. Captain Battles clinging for dear life to his seat, his face like a bobbing lump of grimy suet. A flash of Miss Lee too: hair whipping around her calm face as she sat in the wagon bed, hands gripping a sideboard.

The troopers crashed full tilt into the mass of clawing brush, but they did not penetrate it deeply. O'Hearn's bull voice was roaring over and over an order to halt, dismount, dig in along its edge. As well as rambling clumps of scrub brush, there were massive outcrops and boulders. The men flung themselves out of saddle and did not even wait to secure their mounts. All of them were diving for the nearest shelter.

The Dougherty had almost achieved the thickets when a rear wheel jounced against a boulder and cracked its felloe and rim. The wagon careened wildly, dragged a few more lurching yards by the team's momentum. The wagon box was tilted askew as it hammered to a jarring stop, flinging its occupants hard against a sideboard.

Captain Battles scrambled to his feet and dropped to the ground, ignoring the girl in his clumsy dash for safety. Cresta Lee had been tumbled under her seat in a squirming, momentarily helpless tangle of skirts and frothy petticoat.

Honus, just dismounting, had a dim impulse to rescue her; but young Custer, young Lochinvar, whoever, was in ahead of him. Lieutenant Spingarn swooped his bay alongside the canted wagon and, as Miss Lee was pulling herself upright, plucked her up in the circle of his arm. He spurred on through an alley in the brush; Honus lost sight of them.

The last troopers were vacating their saddles, dropping to kneeling or prone positions behind bushes and rocks. Meantime their frenzied horses went bolting away. One man changed his mind after leaping down—grabbed for his animal's rein. He managed to snare it and swing up. But breaking out of the thickets, he was smashed from his saddle by a hostile bullet.

That was the one and only attempt at escape. The Indians outnumbered the detail several times over, their ponies were fresh. O'Hearn was right. The troop must dig in on the spot, try to put up a game enough fight to discourage the foe.

The Indians came splashing across the river, flinging out silvery jets of water. They came surging up the near bank as O'Hearn shouted for pistols to break the charge.

The troopers' ragged salvo brought down a couple of ponies. None of the braves were hit. The two rendered horseless were swung up behind comrades. The hostiles drew rein, wheeled their mounts, dashed back for the creek.

The charge had been broken quickly, it seemed—but had it?

Though it would be suicidal of them to continue across that open space, the retreat had been too perfectly timed. . . .

They withdrew only to the bank of the river. Dropping off their ponies, they fanned out behind the cutbank, firing back, as well sheltered now as the troopers.

Honus was burrowed in behind a cluster of shattered rock. He was aware of the plowhandle grip of his big service revolver bucking against his palm as he shot at a puff of smoke here, a coppery shoulder there—again at a face smeared with charcoaled grease.

It all seemed oddly unreal, even hallucinatory, yet agonizingly real. He wasn't aware of hitting anything, but in the back of his thoughts burned a small lusty pride that he was tasting his first field action without taking buck fever. He had worried that he might.

Gunroar. Stinking reek of powderfumes. Crazed shoutings and screamings. These became the sum of his world. Off right of him, Menzies crouched, yelling like a deranged man as he pumped bullets. And Sergeant O'Hearn was making the rounds of his dug-in men, ducking his big body in a crouching lope as he ran, here shouting a word of encouragement, there slapping a fear-frozen recruit to a semblance of battle stance.

Honus' hammer fell on an empty chamber: he promptly, mechanically flicked open the loading gate, punched out shell cases, got open his cartridge box, thumbed in fresh bullets—and did not fumble once. He felt a hand fall on his shoulder—"Good lad"—and looked up at O'Hearn. No nervous grimacing now in the big sergeant's gaunt face. It was lighted by a fighting grin and a look of exalted frenzy such as an old Norse berserker might have worn.

It got to Honus. He cooled: squeezed off his next rounds carefully.

Now O'Hearn was yelling for them to bring rifles into play. Somewhere Lieutenant Spingarn was also shouting commands, but a frantic blurring nullified them; only the sergeant's bullboom was reaching the men.

The ritual of war, Honus thought: earing back the hammer

21

of his rifle, firing, working the trapdoor action, loading, shooting again. His shoulder was bruised by the shattering recoil of steel buttplate; the barrel grew hot, hotter, under his hands.

This, at last, was The Enemy. Belchings of whitish smoke obscured almost everything, yet scatterings of icy detail rocked against his brain. The Enemy. Bright warbonnets—warshirts tasseled with scalplocks—terribly painted faces. Details . . .

He began to notice a difference in the tempo of shooting. Their own firing had slacked off, but not the Indians'.

The troopers had broken the horse charge with their six-shooters: Colt .45's newly issued to replace the old Remington, Starr and Colt .44's. Once they had switched to rifles, a jarring contrast hit the ear.

The Indians had used long guns from the start, everything from ancient trade muskets to modern weapons. But most of them, Honus realized, were getting off many times the rounds that the cavalrymen were in the same space. . . .

The troopers were armed well enough, come to that. The big 1873 Springfields, standard issue, were powerful, hard-hitting guns. But also, to many a trooper's rue, the .45-.70 "charcoal furnaces" were single shot.

After a while it was suddenly, alarmingly clear that most of the Cheyennes were armed with repeating rifles—no wonder the troopers couldn't match their rate of fire.

Now, though, for some reason, the Indians' shots were dwindling to sporadic bursts. On O'Hearn's order, the troopers held their own fire down, half-waiting.

Honus' palms were scorched. He dug out a bandanna and tore it in strips and wrapped it around his fists. Menzies glanced across; sweat made shining tracks on his blackened face.

He said: "You all right?"

"I think."

Menzies rested his cheek on the crumbling stone, peering out of his raw slitted eyes at the cutbank. "Red devils're up to something. What'n hell?"

Honus didn't have the answer, but the respite gave his methodical brain a chance to click again. He muttered, "Funny."

"What?"

"Why, the way they caught us. I mean, it was good sense to wait till we'd ridden off our morning edge, but hitting us as they did wasn't. They might have caught us in the open any number of places. Instead they chose a spot fairly close to all this brush and rock. Natural cover where they can't hope to drive us out. . . ."

"Ahhh!" Menzies spat. "Who'n hell knows why a blinking reddie does anything?"

"Indians aren't stupid," Honus began flatly. Then let it go. Trying to explain the kinds and degrees of human intelligence to Menzies' caliber of clabber-brain was worse than useless.

He thought hard. The Cheyenne maneuver must mask some strategy. If . . .

The glimmer of an answer touched him even before the slow warm breeze pressing their backs brought his nostrils an acrid hint of smoke. The Cheyennes had fired the brush.

An outbreak of apprehensive mutters rippled through the men. The Indians in the cutbank threw out taunting yips.

Fire. Threat of it seized a man's brain with a fear that was primordial, unreasoning. It was the instinctive fear of the primal creature, of any child who has picked up a hot ember unknowingly.

The Cheyenne had set things up adroitly, driving the pony soldiers into the convenient cover of this vast and rambling thicket. Its individual clumps were so dense that separate wands struggled in fierce competition for sun, soil, water, with the result that the whole motte was literally packed with dead brush.

The wind was driving out of the south, not hard but steadily. You couldn't yet see the flames, but now you could hear their crackling whisper, like fresh parchment crumpling. Shadowy trickles of smoke were crawling from the wall of brush. The fire was spreading inexorably to right and left as well as ahead.

Every man knew the bitter choice it forced: run out to be shot down or stay to be roasted alive.

Only there was no choice, really. Not with Sergeant O'Hearn present to strap every man fast to his duty.

The Cheyenne had apparently been waiting for them to demoralize and bolt. When they didn't, the Indians again opened up with a fierce peppering fire. "Stand steady," boomed O'Hearn's firm voice, over and over.

Captain Battles, who had made himself scarce, came scrambling suddenly out of the deeper thickets. O'Hearn had sheltered behind an outcrop a short distance from Honus, and Battles scurried like a fat scared rabbit from the brush and dropped beside the sergeant. The fishbelly blob of the captain's face was streaked with dirt and tears.

"My God . . . fire?"

"Yes, sir. Best get out your sidearm, Captain. We'll want to muster every gun we—"

"Where's Spingarn?" Battles chattered. "Where is that stupid blunderhead? All his doing—all of this—"

"Don't know where the lieutenant'd be, sir. But it was my doing, if anyone's. I give the order to dig in here."

"It was Spingarn," Battles mumbled. "Oh, that idiot. That cocky, stupid idiot."

He began to sob like a tired child, tears crawling muddily down his cheeks. Honus Gant knew that vague sick horror that comes to a soldier seeing the symbol of his leadership wilting, crumbling.

O'Hearn's big fists seized Battles by the collar, shaking him. The captain's chins wobbled; his nerveless body trembled like a sack of warm grease.

"Goddammit, sir, you're an officer! You got an example to set these men!"

Battles pawed vaguely at O'Hearn's hands. "We can treat with them, Sergeant." His eyes were a madman's. "White flag—"

"God, sir!" O'Hearn roared the words. "Don't you understand? This here is a massacre! Them bloody butchers want nothing but our hides. And Mary's blessed son help any man of us they take alive!"

"No. Talk. They . . . we talk. Make 'em listen—"

Battles broke the sergeant's hold and sprang to his feet and ran out to the open. He shouted and waved his hands. He pulled his pistol and held it above his head, and then threw it away. He ran toward the Indians, shrieking inarticulately.

The Cheyennes held their fire till he was only yards from the cutbank. Then his body jerked to the impact of a dozen bullets; he went down in full run, skidding on his face in the grass.

Six or seven braves leaped on their ponies and came charging up from the bottoms at a whooping run. They thundered past the prone body. It quivered flaccidly as the flint-shod lances were buried in its back. The Indians circled back and tightly ringed the corpse, yanking the lances out and plunging them in repeatedly. They were venting a pure contempt on the body. More than physical triumph, this was a moral victory. Here was a chief of pony soldiers and his heart had been rotten.

There was a demonic horror about the tableau that had held the troopers paralyzed. O'Hearn, muttering a curse, was the first to recover. He shot one of the braves off his pony. An echoing roar of carbines now from the other troopers sent the Indians wheeling back to shelter with derisive yells.

By now the cherry flicker of flames could be glimpsed, driving behind the quickening spirals of smoke. The wind carried waves of heat against the men's bodies. They all knew it would quickly worsen: the unreasoning panic came flooding back.

Green wands that mingled with the old dry brush began to smoke, erupting great greasy billows across the area now, blinding the men, making them cough harshly.

This was what the Cheyennes had waited for.

They came surging up over the cutbank's lip in a broken line, but for the moment all that the gagging, watery-eyed troopers could make out was a phalanx of riderless ponies rushing at them. Then they saw that the Indians were hanging low on their mounts' off flanks, each supporting himself one-handed by a horsehair rope woven into his pony's shaggy mane and by a leg slung over the animal's back, while he fired from under its neck.

They swept across the open ground toward the soldiers, howling and shooting. This time the charge was savage, concerted, implacable as a juggernaut. This time it would not be turned back. . . .

Chapter Three

Cresta Marybelle Lee was a very practical, very tough-minded girl. She had learned in early childhood about life's ungentle ironies. Of her mother, who had died when she was four, she had only the dimmest memory.

Her father she remembered only too well—a funny bearded giant of a man with a black eyepatch and a booming laugh that hid a core of fear and indecision. She hadn't cared: to her he was the center of all kindness and gentleness; she had adored everything about him, even the heavy scent of cloves he constantly chewed to cover his constant drinking.

When Cresta was eight, he had gone away, leaving her with friends and a promise to return quickly. After a few months the friends had sent her to an orphanage. She never saw her father again.

Cresta Lee had learned several mature bits of business at a tender age. For example, that she could keep herself from feeling anything that she did not want to feel. For another, that one should seize opportunity as it came, that if it did not one should promote it in every way possible or else bide one's time for as long as necessary.

That philosophy had brought her a long way in the four short years since she had left the orphanage at fourteen. It had finally gotten her, at eighteen, engaged to the scion of one of Beacon Hill's oldest families.

Even then she had not indulged in any self-congratulatory puffs. She had learned well the lesson that the gods raised hope only to dash it capriciously. That one bad break could wipe out years of work and planning.

Therefore Cresta Lee hadn't wasted time or tears on futile regrets after her capture by Spotted Wolf's band. She had accepted it for the bad break it was, and just as promptly had begun to plan for the day of her escape.

It had taken her two patient, unhurried years, during which she had set herself to mastering her captors' language, customs and plains lore. Since the band was constantly on the move, she was able to map the whole Platte River region in her mind. She knew landmarks, waterholes, places where heavy cover was, and where there was none. She knew where the Pine Hills Agency was, for the band had sometimes camped within distant view of its buildings.

Meantime she had pretended—not meekness, for that was beyond her—a simple acceptance of her lot. The Cheyennes had gradually relaxed their vigilance with her. Why not? Other white women had given up, adjusted to their captors' ways, become Indian in heart and mind.

What they could not know was the fine-steel quality of Cresta Lee's self-intactness, reinforced by the tireless planning that occupied her thoughts. Finally it was just a matter of finding the chance . . . the good break.

One night the band bivouacked on a nameless creek some twenty miles north of the agency. She had left camp ostensibly to fetch wood, a water bottle of horsegut and some jerky tied from her waist under her buckskin dress.

She hadn't struck due southward at first. Spotted Wolf would expect her to make for the agency. Nobody's fool, Spotted Wolf—he knew she was clever. But she was also white and a woman; he would not look for too grand a performance. So she had headed roughly east, leaving a fairly evident and slightly panicky trail with a few clumsy attempts at concealment to demonstrate to the Cheyenne trackers that she hadn't a notion where she was going and was already thoroughly lost—and finally had blundered herself quite purposefully into a region of rock and woody cover. Here she'd set about losing herself in earnest, and successfully.

Afterward she had skirted in a careful, miles-long circle that was full of patient detours, traveling stretches of open country only by night. It had taken her a full week to reach the agency. . . .

Cresta Lee had endured a long captivity, trying days of flight, keeping an iron composure through it all. But she thought she might be nearing the end of it.

After lifting her from the disabled wagon and carrying her back to the relative safety of the deeper thickets, Lieutenant Spingarn had abandoned gallantry. He had practically dumped her to the ground in the middle of the dense chaparral, then had turned his mount without a word and headed back for the melee where, presumably, all glory was.

Cresta had crouched where he left her for long moments, listening to the rattle of gunfire, shrillness of war cries.

Of all cruel blows in her young life—and there'd been more than enough—this one was the worst.

She'd barely had a glimpse of the attackers, but they must be Spotted Wolf and his Dog Soldiers. No other hostile force in hundreds of square miles, she knew that—and Spotted Wolf, though his band wasn't large, could muster enough braves to outnumber the small paymaster's detail four to one.

He would overrun the troopers quickly. Then the Cheyennes would beat these thickets to make sure no pony soldier had eluded them. She would be discovered.

Indecision—her father's special weakness—had no place in Cresta's life. The Cheyennes rarely took captives. And she had escaped them once—humiliated their best trackers into the bargain. They wouldn't take her alive a second time.

Pushing to her feet, she plunged back through the thickets. Away from the tumult of shots and shouts. She had to ram her way through the tight growth. Its brambly fingers plucked at her loose hair and ripped her dress. Again and again she had to drop to hands and knees and worm beneath the fountain-ing masses of brush. Her skirt and pettiskirt were quickly reduced to shreds.

It seemed a long time before the brush began to thin out ahead of her. A gradual maze of corridors opened up between the clumps. She was able to slip easily between them.

She was half-running when she came to the edge of a deep swale. The brush ended in straggling fingers halfway to its bottom.

Beyond rose a boulder-studded rise which rounded away into undulant vistas of yellow grass pocked by more boulders and brush. Seeing the stark prospect ahead made Cresta pull up short, considering her chances. They weren't good.

Escape from the Cheyennes would still mean being stranded on the plains without food or water, without a weapon or a horse. Before, she had survived for a week on a little jerky and water, a good knowledge of the country—and (she wasn't deceiving herself) a large quota of luck. But she had only a sketchy knowledge of this area to the east and south and not an inkling of where to find food, water or good cover. Matters that made a sobering difference.

A few of the troopers might escape the Cheyenne trap—though she doubted it. But a few together would stand a better chance of getting out alive. Working together, they might even be able to recapture some of the saddle mounts and pack animals that had gotten away—another forlorn hope, she had to admit.

Well, no harm in waiting to find out—but not here at the perimeter of the thickets. She would be safer a little distance off.

Cresta trotted down the slope, holding the remains of her skirt well above her feet. She lost no time cutting across the little swale and up the long rocky rise opposite. She could find shelter and a good vantage point at its summit. . . .

She was far short of the top when the noise of horses reached her. Cresta twisted one glance over her shoulder, saw nothing, and made for a flat massive rock that shelved out of the hillflank. She dropped almost prone behind it, bracing her slightly raised weight with her hands so she could peer over it. The sun-blasted stone was uncomfortably hot even through her clothing and the smooth callus of her palms.

The horsemen swept into sight around a slow curve of hill— a small party of Cheyennes holding flaming oil-soaked branches well away from their bodies. They rode halfway along the facing slope where the thickets ended, their purpose evident even before the first brave flung his torch into a dead clump.

Cresta's heart clotted in her throat. She had slipped out of the trap only in time.

She knew the warrior leader at once: he wore a familiar wolfskin around his shoulders, a beautiful warbonnet of white eagle feathers. The sorrel stallion he rode was magnificent, a proudly gaited brute whose coat was turned to a red-gold blaze by the sun.

But the rider himself—tall, splendidly muscled, straight as a war arrow even in his late middle years—was a match for his mount. Shouting commands, his voice had the dignity of a drumroll.

"*Hone-ehe-hemo*," Cresta whispered. Spotted Wolf . . . of course. His fine hand was visible in this whole strategy.

One by one, spreading out widely, the braves pitched their brands into the brush. For a few moments the flames made small avid cracklings. Then the tinder-dry clumps exploded, one after another, into pyres of flame. Spotted Wolf turned his pony and led the whooping party back toward the battle.

Cresta Lee watched a slight wind fan the flames to sucking torrents that leaped from one clump to the next. The fire was racing into the central mass of dry brush. Nothing could stop it now.

Chapter Four

Honus' eyes stung and watered; his throat was rasped raw by coughing. He tried to catch a decent sight of the enemy through the sullen veils of drifting smoke that had suddenly obscured everything.

At the last moment of their charge, the Cheyennes had divided cleanly and thundered to either side of the troopers like a splitting wave. Using their horsehair support ropes and clinging to their ponies' off flanks, they were almost completely hidden. The troopers shot at the ponies. Several went down in kicking tangles. The rest passed by into the surging smoke and massed brush, and were cut off.

Their intention was clear: to infiltrate to the sides and rear of the trapped soldiers.

Honus' smoke-stung eyes had blurred till he could hardly see at all, but he went on doggedly reloading and firing. His briefly acquired taste for battle had curled up in his guts like a shriveled memory.

Pandemonium on every side. The Indians had abandoned their ponies. They were slithering in among the choking, blinded troopers like deadly shadows.

Honus could make out hardly any of it in the sun-yellowed fog of smoke mingled with dust raised by running ponies. All unreal again: men all along the fringes of the motte locked in weird swaying battle, like actors in a misty chimera. The Cheyennes were everywhere, their cries triumphantly shrill and raking.

Menzies wheeled toward him. "No chance here! Best we run for it, devil take the hindmost—"

A Cheyenne forced his pony in a crashing lunge through the brush to their left. He sprang to the ground almost at Menzies' side. A steel hatchet glittered high in the saffron air, descended. The blade was buried in Menzies' skull before he could even twist to face his opponent, let alone bring up his rifle.

The hand ax stuck fast as the trooper's body toppled sideways. The slippery handle was wrenched from the Indian's fist. He spun on his heel, a hunting knife flashing from its sheath, and leaped at Honus Gant.

Honus was on his feet, a shell chambered, rifle hammer thumbed back. The Indian was almost on him—a lean coppery breechclouted figure whose charcoaled face was scoured to a feral wildness—when he fired. The side of the Cheyenne's face dissolved in a bloody mask. He fell across Menzies' body.

A violent trembling seized Honus. His breakfast clawed up in his throat like hot bile. Till now he had shot at anonymous figures. Killing a man under your nose was death's reality. Raw and stinking death whose livid freckling was on his shirt and hands.

Devil take the hindmost. O'Hearn's boom was stilled. The remaining troopers were fighting their way into the deeper brush, popping wildly at their enemies or desperately hacking with empty rifles at coup-hungry adversaries. Most of them had pulled to a defensive group. A mistake, for the Cheyennes converged on the lot- at once.

Honus—luckily for him—was cut off from the rest. And for the moment found himself totally ignored, the shroud of smoke and dust proving a sudden benison. Escape. There was nothing else now.

He plunged away into the heart of the brush. He had a dim notion of penetrating it as close to the flames as he could bear—reasoning that nobody else would think of braving the intense heat nor expect him to—at an angle that would bring him out well away from the concentration of Cheyennes.

Wild shots riddled the underbrush; several kicked up geysers of dirt close to Honus' legs. He wove his way through the smoky chaos by feel and by instinct, seeking slender breaks between the thickets. His eyes were raw swimming blurs, his bearings gone, but the shooting was falling behind him. He might yet make it. . . .

He was getting close—too close—to the raging wall of flame. The surges of heat washed against his body with a blistering fury now. He found it was impossible to follow along the fire's edge: it was moving too fast, shooting out irregular fiery arms into the unfired brush.

Honus ducked sideways along its path as best he could, his eyes watery wells of pain, retching on the smoke he had swallowed. At one terrifying moment he thought he had charged into the very middle of it. The windy flames roared all around him, flapping like rusty banners in the pitchy billows. The heat nearly made him scream. Running almost totally blind, he slashed frenziedly at the smoking thickets with his rifle and free hand. Sparks flew. Inadvertently he seized a burning switch: it clung and ate into his flesh. Yelling, he smeared the glowing splinters off on his trousers.

Suddenly he pitched out of the fiery thickets. He was through. A gust of good air hit his face. He was past the fire now, past the worst of the brush but not yet out of it.

Caution flagged him to a halt.

He was gagging sickly on the smoke that had clawed his eyes raw; he could feel every throb of his heart in his scorched hand. Just beyond the fiery perimeter where he stood, it was still agonizingly hot, and in a few minutes more the remaining motte would erupt into a vast torch.

But the enemy might be waiting for him out there. He could spare the few seconds needed to clear his eyes and get his rifle loaded. And try to get an idea what he would face next.

He breeched a fresh shell while he blinked his eyes till the landscape took watery form: curving swells of land that fell away to the horizon.

Honus moved cautiously out of the thickets now, but held to the rambling fringe of them as he pushed south at a trot. To be caught in the open would be fatal. Here, if he picked up the approach of riders, he could take instant refuge in the brush and blowing curtain of smoke. He would hold south along the brush to its farthest extent. . . .

Soon the thickets began to dwindle; he followed their curving edge inward, almost to the charred area where the fire had been started. His vision was clearer now. No sign of the enemy. The little shooting that kept up was far to his back.

He was descending a hill into a swale, and he braced his muscles for a quick sprint up the rocky open hill opposite. Then he came to a dead stop, staring.

Somebody hidden among the gaunt sprawl of boulders a short distance upslope had stood up. Miss Cresta Lee, no less. Straight, diminutive, and apparently unhurt, the brown tatters of her skirt feathering in the wind. She waved a hand at him.

Honus felt a quick guilt: he had completely forgotten the girl. He supposed all of them had.

A sound snatched his attention. Hoofs pounding over soft earth as a rider came this way along the motte's edge.

All that Honus could do was melt to the ground and squirm under some low-growing brush. It should conceal him if the man didn't pass too closely. Cresta Lee had already dopped behind her rock again.

A Cheyenne brave came into sight, nudging his mount along in a slow circuit of the thicket, which he was evidently patrolling for escapees. Suddenly he hauled up, his eyes intent on the hillside.

Honus had a good view of the scape even from his cramped vantage. Now he saw what the brave had seen. The brown smudge of Cresta Lee's skirt hem showing at the edge of the boulder that hid her. Enough to seize a plains warrior's eye.

"Hai!"

The Cheyenne kicked his pony around, tearing up clods as he sent the animal up the rise in a stretching run.

The girl sprang to her feet and ran like a deer, cutting away at right angles along the slope. The flapping 'tatters of dress and petticoat hampered her. The brave emitted a laughing yip and swung to cut her off.

Honus scrambled from beneath his bush and came up on one knee, leveling his rifle. He followed the Indian, lined him along the sights, pulled trigger.

The 405-grain bullet slammed into the slight body of the brave like a giant fist and wiped him from his saddle, rolling him over and over like a bundle of rags. His horse bolted away.

Honus went up the hill at a stumbling run. When he reached Cresta Lee, she had relieved the dead Cheyenne of a beaded belt with a hatchet and sheath knife. The Indian's rifle was gone with his horse, secure in a buckskin scabbard.

"Any more of you coming?"

Honus felt that numb shock again, meeting her eyes. They were as untroubled as a child's—and not from the calm that masks hysteria.

"Uh? Er—no, I don't think so. At least I, uh, didn't see any more of our men—"

"All right. Follow me." She spoke over her shoulder; she was already moving away.

"No," Honus said hoarsely. "Not yet. If—"

She halted and looked at him, her brows drawing down. "Listen," she said. "Just listen."

He did.

The shooting had tapered away. There was no sound but the steady snap and crackle of flames, and beyond that an occasional exulting whoop.

It was over for N Troop. For green recruit and seasoned campaigner alike. Over because of Cheyenne strategy. Because everyone knew the reddies would never attack a paymaster. Because chance had thrown together on a single detail two bad officers—an errant coward and an irresponsible fool. . . .

"Come on now," Cresta Lee said sharply. "There's nothing

you can do. When they find this one and read the sign they'll be looking for us. Come on! . . ."

Nothing you can do. Mechanically Honus fumbled a fresh load into his rifle, and followed her.

She struck into the shallow roll of ridges to the south, moving in a patient, zigzag course. Dully he saw that she moved with an Indian's quick noiseless ease, picking her way over patches along the deep curves of hill where wind or water had torn away sod and soil, exposing gravel and solid shale. A tracker might pick up their spoor with difficulty, but he would be hours following it up.

Had any besides the girl and himself broken out of the trap? It was possible. But not likely. Even if any had, they wouldn't stand a chance without horses. The Cheyennes would run them down quickly on the open plain.

Cresta Lee halted deep in a field of giant splintered boulders.

"We can lay low here," she said quietly. "My guess is that they'll look for us—but not very long or hard. Spotted Wolf won't want to waste the time."

"Spotted Wolf—you're sure this was . . ."

"I saw him."

She settled down on her heels between the gargantuan slabs of rock and folded her arms across her knees. Honus sat down beside her, feeling cold in his guts in spite of the intense reflected heat of the boulders. He stared at the greasy pall of smoke rising above the burning thicket one thousand yards away.

A sharp, involuntary groan left him. What were they doing now? Dispatching the wounded with lance and knife? Looting? He knew that they rarely took prisoners. . . .

Cresta Lee closed her fingers over his arm. "Don't even think about it," she said.

"About what?"

"Going back there now. Nothing you can do, understand? *Nothing.*"

Honus stared at her face. Fine beads of sweat pearled her golden skin. Otherwise her face was so cool and opaque, it might have been a mask . . . just a mask. *Does she have any feelings at all?* He shook her hand away.

The boulder field was like a furnace. Sweat puddled in his boots; his clothes were wet dirty rags. His eyes ached from the pounding glitter of sun pouring down on naked rock.

Dead, he thought. *All dead.* And he was wearing only a few scratches and a burn on his hand. He felt almost traitorous. Yet the fight had turned to a rout at the last, and none had thought of anything but escape.

"They were after you," he said bitterly. "All of this because you—"

"That's a lot of bull," snapped Cresta Lee. "They weren't after me."

"Well, you escaped from them. And no Army paymaster has been attacked by Indians . . . not till today. What else could it be?"

"I don't know. But don't lay this to my account, Mister. In the first place, they wouldn't make up an elaborate trap like this one just to recover a runaway—now would they? In the second—they couldn't have known I was with this detachment to begin with. . . ."

"They must have seen you in the attack!"

"In the wagon from a distance—sure. Dressed as just another white woman. That's what they saw. Only that one you did for saw me up close. Which, as far as I can see, doesn't make a hell of a lot of difference."

"Not to you, apparently," Honus muttered. "Though you'd be safe enough if they did find us, come to that."

"Bull," Cresta Lee said in an unruffled tone. "I don't know what they'd do to me, but it'd be the worst, for sure. Maybe even the burning pole. I not only ran away, I outguessed the trackers who were sent after me. None of which did much for their pride. Least of all Spotted Wolf's. I think . . ." She paused, almost reflectively. "I really think he'd kill me."

"Because of *pride?*"

"Just that." She gave him that wise, cool look. "I was his wife."

38

Chapter Five

It seemed an eternity later that they heard the Cheyennes' last fierce yips of victory trailing in the afternoon distance, as they pounded away toward the south. And a long time after that before the cautious Miss Lee said it was all right to leave the boulder field.

They trudged back to the scene of massacre. . . .

Honus saw total carnage. The vast brush motte had been reduced to ash and char except for a few stripped blackened wands nudging up forlornly here and there. The flames were dying out except at the fringes where orange tongues still licked sporadically at clots of shrubbery. Tatters of smoke curled up in the sunlight, which blazed them to a satiny fog.

Ever practical, Cresta Lee went off by herself to scout the area for anything useful that might be salvaged.

Honus moved across the hot ground like a gaunt plodding zombie. Pallid ash puffed under his boots. He hadn't seen the like of this in his twenty-five years. A scene from a passive inferno. He tramped past the sprawled bodies of men with whom he'd shared barracks and mess table and the light of a hundred campfires. He had been close to only a few. But all had played a part in the sights and sounds of everyday.

He felt the same sad and terrifying jolt of gut-sickness at

each different face he looked on, unable to shake the conviction that he, by all rights, should be lying here with the rest. Dead by lance or bullet. Crumpled in a grotesque posture in the smoking shreds of his uniform. He did not want to see and absorb these sights, yet could not keep himself from it. As if the scene had to be forcibly seared into his brain.

He felt a dim surprise that the bodies bore almost no signs of mutilation. He guessed it was true, what his friend the old scout had said—snorting at the atrocity tales created by sensational journalism and spread by scatterbrains. The plains warriors didn't torture. "They takes scalps," the old man had told him, "and they cuts off a dead enemy's left arm, maybe only the left hand. Just that. Gets their name from that. Cheyenne means 'Cut-Arm People.' . . ."

A few wanton mutilations showed here and there. Probably inflicted by the handful of sadistic imbeciles that infested any army. The late N Troop had contained a few such men.

He found Lieutenant Rufus Spingarn, dashing Indian fighter, slumped on the ground with his back against a boulder, the front of his pretty blue double-breasted miner's shirt soaked with darkly drying blood. His head was sunk on his chest, a breeze stirred his dark curly hair.

Honus remembered hearing that the Indians had not taken Yellow Hair Custer's scalp either—some said out of respect, others because he had died badly, and who in hell could read an Injun's reasons? The Cheyennes might have noticed Spingarn's resemblance to his idol. . . .

But there was no way of really telling how the lieutenant or any of them had died. Along with the bodies of their own dead, the Cheyennes had carried off all the troopers' weapons; the cartridge boxes had been torn from their belts. Pieces of uniforms had been scavenged from bodies untouched by the fire.

A little farther on, Honus found O'Hearn.

The sergeant had been scalped, left arm taken; the flint head of a snapped-off lance was buried in his chest. Otherwise he looked as if he had lain down to sleep, his face toughly serene. The fighting grin seemed to hover like a contented shadow on his mouth. No need to question how he had died.

In spite of the sick horror gripping him, Honus moved from body to body in a kind of frozen dogged calm. It wasn't till he came on Menzies again, crumpled under the body of the first Cheyenne downed by Honus, that something snapped in him.

Honus felt his eyes start to blur. "I'm sorry," he whispered.

He was. Sorry that he hadn't warmed to a real appreciation of Menzies' friendship, ashamed of the small secret contempt he had felt at the man's crudeness and other lacks. For Menzies had been very much a man in the final and best sense: that was what counted.

It did no good to be sorry. But saying the words aloud let Honus give vent to the anguish that lay behind the madness still chilling his brain.

He prowled aimlessly across the scorched ground, the welling guilty grief changed to anger now. He tramped wildly through the ashes and rubble, kicking at any small burned object.

"What *are* you doing, for God's sake?"

Cresta Lee's caustic query shocked him back to himself.

He came to a halt, blinking at her. She stood a few yards off, fists on her hips, small and sturdy in the limp tatters of her dress, looking totally out of patience.

"Nothing. I was . . ." He let the words trail.

"Well, just snap to now, will you? We've things to do if we want to get out of this with whole skins. I've been looking around. They didn't leave a lot, but there should be a few articles we can use. So let's . . . are you listening?"

Honus gave her a dull stare. "We have to bury them."

"What! Are you crazy? Only thing we have to do is take what we need and clear out of here!"

Her snappish indignation was a bellows pumping at the live coal of his anger. "Don't you have any decent feelings?"

"Decent is as decent does. Back there"—she gave a small contemptuous nod toward the East and Civilization—"it may mean something. Out in this place, let me tell you, it doesn't mean one damned thing. All that counts is staying alive."

She leaned forward a little from the waist, fists braced on her hips. "And soldier—I mean to stay alive. I slaved and planned two years to get away from them. Now I'm out of it halfway—still free anyhow—and you're not putting me back in it with your damned foolishness! We're way out on the shaggy end of nowhere, and we're going to need each other. Not that you're much, but you have enough nerve, I guess—you can shoot a little. I'm getting out all the way. And you're going to help me."

Honus' jaw had been hardening slowly as she talked, and now a rich crawl of heat was edging up toward his hair, washing out the freckles. Honus Gant was getting madder than he had ever been in his life.

Miss Cresta Lee saw this very plainly. And wisely held her tongue. She watched him warily.

With a great effort, Honus choked down his rage. He had been taught to speak softly to a woman, even if she had a shrewish tongue and an indecent vocabulary, and was, by all odds, the most cold-blooded female he had ever met.

Also his good bedrock of common sense was asserting itself. It was a family trait—one which Honus' great-aunt Maddie, the wonderful old lady who had raised him, had taken pains to cultivate in him.

Cresta Lee was obnoxious, but she was right.

They had escaped the Cheyennes, but their position was still far from cozy. They were miles from any civilized post that either one knew of, and no matter which way they went, they faced a foot journey of many long, possibly dangerous miles. In these circumstances, they had no duty to the dead . . . only themselves.

"All right," Honus said wearily. "We're about halfway between the Pine Hills Agency and Fort Reunion . . . but a little nearer Reunion, I'd say. There are probably a few ranches that are nearer yet, but I couldn't swear to finding them—and if we stick to the road, we can't get lost."

Cresta Lee nodded coolly. "Only we'll follow the road till it splits away from the river. Then we'll follow the river. . . ."

"Miss Lee, that's not a wise thought—"

"Look, Janroe River swings way north and then swings back, doesn't it, by Fort Reunion?"

"Of course, but that's my point. The road runs almost straight to Reunion. The river makes that huge loop." The inanity of this bickering—here and now—struck him. But a dull stubborn residue of his anger seemed to push at him. "We'd walk half again as far to reach the same place!"

"Use your head," Cresta Lee snapped. "If Spotted Wolf has taken to making attacks along this road, anybody on it— particularly small parties—will be sitting ducks."

"But when Captain Battles' paywagon fails to arrive on schedule, they'll send out troops to learn what's amiss. They'll meet us—"

"How soon?"

"Well—" A lame pause. "I'd imagine in a few days. . . ."

"By which time we could be most of the damned distance to the fort. Look—" She raised her left hand, the fingers out-fanned, and ticked them off one by one. "All along the Janroe, there's heavy brush and cover. Get wind of danger and you can find shelter in no time. There's trees here and there, shade when the sun gets fierce. There's food for the picking—bushes loaded with wild plums and berries. A good chance we can scare up a jackrabbit or two. Most important, we're always close to water. So—" She let the hand drop in a flat, unequivocal gesture. "You do what you want, Buster. I'm following the river all the way."

She had already turned in that quick imperative way, tossing the last words across her shoulder as she moved off.

The two of them went carefully over the ashy ground, hunting for anything that might be of use. They didn't find much. Cresta Lee located her wide straw hat that had been blown off when the attack came, hung up in a snag of brush by the creek. She also found one of the blue orange-bordered army blankets trampled in the muddy creekbank. It was badly scorched, partly chopped to ribbons, but after she had done a trimming job with her knife, the remainder made a serviceable skirt, knotted around her waist. Honus found a dented canteen which a bullet had passed through. A couple of wooden plugs would make it usable.

The pack animals that had stampeded might have been rounded up by the raiders, or they might still be running. In either case, they were gone and so were the grub supplies they carried. General Crook, now in charge of the Army's Department of the Platte, had had the troops under his command abandon their heavy baggage and ammunition wagons in favor of pack horses or mules. This ensured the mobility and swiftness essential to pursuing the red foe, but in this case it also emphasized the sobering plight of two survivors. . . .

They searched the Dougherty wagon, which had been overturned and the wheels smashed. The fire had licked at and blackened its hull, but it was still intact otherwise. However, the Indians had stripped it of the little baggage stored inside.

Even the steel-reinforced payroll chest was gone, Honus was surprised to find. Money in gold or greenbacks was supposed to mean nothing to hostiles—yet they had taken the trouble to unload and probably secure to a travois-drag the heavy locked chest.

The startling fact provoked a startling realization. If this were the first time an Army pay escort had been attacked by Indians, they must have been after nothing more than the money itself.

Spotted Wolf, like most of the great war chiefs, was ordinarily a guerrilla fighter. When you had a small force, poor logistics, limited firepower, you made the hit-and-run tactic the basis of your fight. You harassed the enemy, destroyed or carried off his supplies, in a war of attrition, not of clear-cut victory.

Today's hard-pressed battle and massacre was a total departure for Spotted Wolf. His stratagem had been, as always, immaculate—but no matter how he'd gone about overwhelming a well-armed detachment of U. S. Cavalry, he would have been bound to pay a bloody price. As he had.

He must have been willing to pay it to get his hands on that paychest. But why?

"Come on," Cresta Lee said impatiently.

They moved off from the wagon, continuing their search. But Honus' scanning of the sooty earth was mechanical: his real attention was grappling with a question which he felt was more important than his safety or Cresta Lee's.

His boot kicked something half-buried in the flaky char.

He bent and picked it up. A rifle. The steel barrel had gotten bent so badly, it had been discarded.

It was one of the repeating rifles the Indians had used. A '73 Model Winchester with, he had heard, a lever action so smooth that you could get off all fifteen loads in as many seconds.

Honus turned it thoughtfully in his hands. He said: "Did Spotted Wolf's men have many guns like this—repeaters—before you left?"

Cresta Lee shrugged. "A few."

"But not many?"

"I said a few." She gave him a level stare. "Nothing like as many as they had today, if that's what you mean."

"It is." Honus scowled. "Where did they get so many spanking-new repeaters all at once? Ordinarily they pick up one here, one there, from settlers or pilgrims they've waylaid. . . ."

"So?"

"I'm thinking of what it could mean . . . a good-sized band of renegades all armed with rifles like this one. Spotted Wolf might have more in mind than just another little rising to harass settlers and make the Army mad. He might . . ."

Honus paused. The two facts clicked into place like safe tumblers. "That's it," he said softly. "No doubt of it. He's found a source of new weapons. The source has to be . . . white men. The paymaster's chest is for *them!*"

"I suppose so."

"But didn't you see anything while you were with them? Haven't you any idea . . . ?"

"No. Look, we've found all we're going to here. Let's get

45

going. It's still a couple hours to sunset, and we can cover a good many miles before dark."

Honus looked around him. Men lay dead at this place—unshriven and unburied. The awful fact of it was a silent shout for some word of ceremony . . . man's lonely cry against the inevitable and the unknown. *I am more*, man had cried since time out of mind, *more than an envelope of flesh—*

A thick and sluggish ache filled his throat. What should he say? What could he—after living through a day like this one? Humbly thank the Almighty and pray for the souls of the fallen? He could—but the words would taste of ashes.

A few lines of Tennyson came to mind: they seemed right.

> "'Was there a man dismayed?
> Not though the soldier knew
> Someone had blundered:
> Theirs not to make reply,
> Theirs not to reason why,
> Theirs but to do and die . . .'"

That would do. It would have to do.

Cresta stood a few paces off, watching him strangely. He said, "All right," and started blindly away.

Two alone on a savage plain. Honus Gant. Quiet, proper and unadventurous Ohio farm lad and erstwhile schoolmaster. Cresta Marybelle Lee. Shrewd, tough and ambitious lass from the New York slums. And more lately, runaway wife of a Cheyenne war chief. Two alone—and on foot. With many hot treacherous miles to go. . . .

Chapter Six

For two days they followed the Janroe's meandering summer-shrunk trickle in its wide swing to the northeast. When it began a slow curve back toward the southeast they knew they had completed a third of the journey. For two people who were exhausted and hungry, those remaining miles stretched ahead like a lonely infinity.

On every side was a monotonous roll of molten plains that rose and tilted away to an incredibly vast horizon. Little sign of life but flies and prairie dogs and the rattlesnakes for which you had to keep a ready eye. Now and then a chicken hawk would spiral against the blue-brittle sky. Occasional bands of wild horses could be spotted. Twice, seeing small bands of horsemen, they took refuge in the scrub willow. Indians. Friendly or hostile—they had no way of knowing, and took no chances.

Even if they had been sure of the Indians, they had nothing to trade for the food they needed. The wild plums and choke-cherries that grew in profusion along the bank were still, for the most part, hard and green. Once they made a passable meal off a patch of wild turnips that Cresta found. But Honus drew the line at most of the edible bark and roots and greenery that she consumed matter-of-factly.

He wanted meat. Several times they flushed out jackrabbits and missed some pretty fair shots. Cresta was no kind of shot at all, and Honus, who had a third-class marksman's rating—meaning that he could hit the target three or less times out of ten shots—only made nearer misses.

It being high summer and the nights warm, they had no need of blankets or extra clothing. That was lucky—and so, he had to admit, was Cresta's acquired plains lore, obnoxious as he found the lady.

Why, he glumly wondered again and again, had he followed up that mad impulse of a year ago and wangled a frontier assignment? He'd had a comfortable niche as a messenger and file clerk in the regimental headquarters at Omaha where you were a soldier in name only, even wearing civilian clothes.

Then the impulsive request to a friendly superior—followed by six months of drill and training at Jefferson Barracks and the assignment to Fort Kearsage where he had learned to sit a horse as if it were a horse and not a kitchen chair.

It had probably been the one time in Honus Gant's life that he had succumbed to adventure's call, and he had done nothing but regret it since. Never more than now, with his nightmare reaction to the massacre aggravated by physical wear.

The constraints between Cresta Lee and himself had relaxed enough in two days for them to carry on a little talk, but except on one subject, Honus did not invite talk.

At twenty, this girl was as consistent a fountain of bristling sarcasm and cynicism as he'd ever met. Of social virtues, she had only wit—and hers was wry and acid.

Concerning herself she was guarded, masking her feelings, ignoring any attempt to crack her private wall. Her reaction to the massacre had been totally callous—and she hadn't made any reference to it since.

He didn't know what her personal goals were, but they had to be as unlovely as her disposition.

Honus had never met her Lieutenant McNair, but at first he had admired the young officer's devotion to her. Now he only felt sorry for him.

With the landscape and the company about equally sterile, Honus found his thoughts revolving constantly back to the question of the missing paychest . . . the repeating rifles . . . Spotted Wolf himself.

That whole business had become an obsession with him. He knew it. But he couldn't help personalizing the situation. Partly, he supposed, it was a feeling of irrational guilt for being (as far as he knew) N Troop's sole survivor.

Then he had killed two of the enemy, a fact which caused him no jubilation. He was not a hunter; he found it hard even to kill for food. Chopping off two human lives made an unhappy blot on his brain.

Spotted Wolf. He knew a little about him—in the detached way of any alert greenhorn who kept his mouth shut and his ears open.

And he beleaguered Cresta Lee with questions. She wasn't eager to discuss her life with the Cheyenne leader, and finally she slammed the door on his curiosity. Before she did, though, he had enough answers to fill out a rough picture.

Born a Southern Cheyenne, Spotted Wolf had first won fame for his skill at horse-stealing. Intelligent, thirsty for knowledge, he had attended the agency schools at Red Dog and Darlington. His English, said Cresta Lee, was still perfect. And he had worked—then—to show his people how to take the best, not the worst, from the white world.

Until twelve years ago. When he had seen his father and mother, his wife and two infant sons, murdered at Sand Creek by Chivington and his blood-hungry Colorado Volunteers.

Spotted Wolf's hatred of the whites was no ordinary hatred. It was total and implacable. It was a war to the death. He had been instrumental in Crook's humiliating defeat at the Rosebud; he had been at the Little Big Horn too.

Though Dull Knife, leader of the Northern Cheyenne nation, had ended his long resistance to the whites, Spotted Wolf, his long-time friend and protégé, had sworn to fight to the death. When Dull Knife and the others had yielded to the

Army's demands that they surrender ancestral lands for the reservation at Darlington, Spotted Wolf had broken away.

Strictly a guerrilla fighter (until N Troop), his strikes were minor, stings rather than blows, but they kept the white population grumping and the Army anxious. His successes were never spectacular—only dead certain.

Thus his medicine was adjudged good; his prestige had climbed quickly. Dull Knife's young men had begun to leave reservation and slip north to join Spotted Wolf. The other great Cheyenne war leaders—Little Wolf, White Antelope, Roman Nose—were all out of the fight. Only Spotted Wolf remained to draw the young hotbloods.

What did it mean—a fighting chief doubling his forces and arming them with the finest repeating rifles? That he was working up to more than small harassments, Honus guessed. That unless he were checked, the country was in for a revival of the bloody hostilities that had ended a short year ago. . . .

It was late afternoon of the second day. They had tramped since early dawn, with only a brief noon stop. The sun-cured swells of buffalo grass rolled into the distance like an undulating carpet of gold.

Honus' walk had turned deliberate and slogging, like an automaton's. He had become more of a horse soldier than he'd known. As a boy he had been used to hiking ten miles to school in any kind of weather. A week of this and he might be back in shape. But now the tender ache in his legs was turning to raw and rubbery pain.

He said: "I think we'd better call it a day. . . ."

"No, you ninny," Cresta Lee said in her usual endearing manner. "Not with a good three hours of daylight left. I'm using 'em. You do what you want."

What he wanted to do was something else, but swearing was an art he had never acquired. Lately he was regretting it more and more.

She was probably as tired as he: the early bounce had left her step. He had the idea that she had to keep driving, driving to outlast him. Outlast the man.

Suddenly she grabbed him by the arm. "Look, Buster! Look—"

Honus saw the big lean jack sitting on a hummock some yards to their right. He was looking straight at them and curiously testing the air. Very carefully Honus cocked his rifle and began to raise it.

"No you don't," Cresta Lee hissed. "You've missed all the easy shots. Give me that!"

She wrestled with him for the Springfield. After a half-hearted resistance, Honus let her take it. She held the gun all wrong, aimed it all wrong, shot it all wrong. The jack went zipping off like a whippet.

"Damn, damn and double damn!" She furiously shook the gun in both hands as if it were an erring child. "What the hell is wrong with this damned thing? And what are you looking so bruised about?"

She stood with her feet apart, glaring truculently. She was certainly a feast for the senses in her dilapidated dress that reeked of two days' worth of sweat and dirt and soot. The seams at shoulders and sides had burst from her nubile exertions. Both skirt and army blanket had been reduced to frayed strips flapping around her legs.

"You keep acting as if you never heard a girl swear, for God's sake!"

Actually he had been taken aback by her bad temper—one fault she hadn't displayed till now. "Not a girl like you—like you're supposed to be."

"Oh, bull!"

She smacked the gun into his hands and stalked on in her favorite marching position—several steps ahead of him.

With all the Indians had taught her, Honus thought dourly, you'd think they would have included a rough education on how to follow a man. On the other hand he imagined that even Spotted Wolf would have been hard put to hammer that particular virtue home to Cresta Lee. . . .

"I don't get you," she said suddenly, not looking back at him. "I really don't at all."

"Heh?" he said blankly.

"You're not much like any soldier I've seen. Oh, you talk better than most, but that's not the thing. I was around Army men a good deal when Johnny and I were courting. You're just not the army type. . . ."

"Suppose not," Honus admitted, giving his shoulders a self-conscious twitch. "I grew up on a farm. Aunt Maddie—my great-aunt—raised me after the typhoid took my father and mother. Farming—that was the life for me."

"Then why leave it, Buster?"

"I have a given name," Honus said stiffly.

She gave him a highly ironic glance across her shoulder. "Yes indeed, Mr. Gant. Anyway, you left. . . ."

"Yes," Honus said in a nettled tone. "After Aunt Maddie passed along, the county took over the farm for taxes and sold it at public auction. I had a fair education—first year normal college—and the local school needed a teacher. So I took the job."

"Ha."

"Why 'ha'?"

"Oh, you do have a temper, Buster, Mr. Gant, but I'd say it takes some strong riling. I just can't see you birching the naughty little boys."

"Well." Honus pulled at his nose in mild embarrassment. "I didn't, matter of fact. I tried to reason with them."

Miss Lee gave a brief and deeply sarcastic laugh. "I can see why that job didn't last."

Honus' face was warming. "It didn't last because a cavalry recruiter came to town and talked about opportunity in the service. It sounded ideal—free lodging and board, and I could save all my pay. I wanted to lay by enough to buy back the family farm, and on a teacher's pay it'd take me a lifetime."

"That's the reason you joined the Army?"

"I took it seriously," he said defensively. "I read everything I could on the art of soldiering. Vegetius, de Saxe, von Steuben and de la Valiere—"

He broke off, embarrassed by the incredulous stare she threw back at him. Finally she slowly shook her head and said, "Well, yes. I shouldn't wonder. I'll bet you did just that. Vegetius!"

Honus flushed angrily. "I think you have more gall than— uh, an army mule."

"Gee, that's funny."

With a half-limp in his gait and a growling emptiness in his belly, it took a vast effort of will to hold his mind to everything he had been taught about courtesy to the so-called tender sex. For whatever good it might do, he decided to keep his mouth shut unless talk were imperative.

The sun, arcing down into the brass-colored horizon at their backs, had reddened to a titanic fireball. Their tramping shadows were flung out in formless and exaggerated silhouettes.

Suddenly Cresta Lee came to a dead halt. She said nothing, only pointed. He saw a pale trickle of smoke climbing against the still, blue-gray sky ahead.

"Camp's close to the creek," she said. "About a mile on. That's a white man's fire."

"How do you know?"

Cresta Lee sighed gently. "It's different from an Indian's fire. We'd better go slow, whites or not . . . you can't be sure of anyone out here."

They covered the next three quarters of a mile briskly. They crept up on a rise just above the camp.

The Janroe angled to form a pleasant wedge of land mantled by a handsome grove of old cottonwoods and junipers. There was a camp containing one canvas-topped wagon and a badly smoking fire. It must have been untended for some minutes.

"You see anybody?" Honus asked.

"No. But he's around." Cresta Lee moved boldly forward. "Let's go on down. But you keep that rifle ready, Buster."

"Sure you don't want it?" Honus couldn't resist saying.

"You're real smart, aren't you?"

Walking slowly, they went down the rise and came into the grove.

Close up, the camp still appeared deserted. Four mules were hobbled on the thick lush bottom grass under the trees. They raised their heads and back-flapped their ears with a kind of lackadaisical hostility, and went on grazing.

"Don't like the smell of this," Cresta Lee said.

Honus turned slowly on his heel. He scanned the cool green shield of undergrowth along the base of the trees. It would pretty well mask anyone who was in hiding. And somebody probably was.

Of course the camper(s) could be out hunting for (his, their) supper. It was just that a ghostly tingle along Honus' spine said otherwise.

"Lord declare," said a man's voice. "If tain't a young lady and a sojer boy. You folks be what you seem, I wonder?"

"Where are you?" Honus awkwardly swept the screen of foliage with his Springfield.

"You find out billy-be-damn quick, boy, you don't put down that cannon. I got a slick ole buffler gun laid square on your gizzard. You lay that there thing down and you turn your backs, both."

"Probably a bluff," Cresta Lee said clearly.

"Bless my raddled old bones, if that ain't a pert little prairie hen you got yourself, sojer." The voice chilled. "You hyper now, boy. I can kill you from here, easy as not."

Chapter Seven

Honus had no intention of getting shot to test Cresta Lee's theory. He laid the Springfield on the ground and about-faced. After a few stubborn moments she pivoted around too, a pure mulishness in her face. Honus knew she would have loved to try something, but was too careful for that.

He strained to catch a rustle of bushes, a scrape of boot—any sound at all. He nearly jumped out of his own boots when somebody spoke from behind him, not a yard away.

"You c'n turn about."

They did.

Honus saw the oddest figure of a man he had ever set eyes on. Not at all thickset, he was short and gnurly enough to seem so. He stood hardly five inches above five feet. There was something simian in his long and powerful arms and short bowed legs. He had a face like a bawdy elf's—wide and ruddy, full of sly smiling wrinkles. His eyes were smooth-worn slate. His hair was a piebald off-color; it was neither flat nor bristly, but burred softly around his ears and temples like a mouse's fur.

He wore a battered horsethief hat, a baggy black suit that was dirty and wrinkled, and knee-high moccasins. His age—indeterminate.

"We were on our way to Fort Reunion," Honus said. "My troop was wiped out. Cheyenne. We were a paymaster's escort. This young lady was on her way to join her fiancé at Reunion."

The man's black-barreled Sharps lowered a little: he carried it as casually as an extra arm. "Massacree, hey?"

Honus nodded. "I'm Private Gant. This is Miss Lee."

"Cumber. Isaac Quinn Cumber. Q. Cumber, y'all get it?" His smile was vast and toothy; his wrinkles meshed into sly and ludicrous prominence. "My daddy had a great ole humor. Lord declare. Y'all sit down and tell me about it. Sit."

It was not an invitation.

Cumber chortled deeply, apropos of nothing, as he kicked up the smoking fire and bent to feed it dry sticks. His rifle, held one-handed, never wavered off them. He moved with a forward apelike roll, carrying his weight athletically on the balls of his feet.

"Heard that shot you let off away back. Left the fire smoking to pull you in. Wanted a sight of you. Heh heh."

He eased down on his haunches across the fire from them. Honus told him about the slaughter of N Troop and the theft of the paychest.

"Well well well well. Ain't that a plumb bob into hell now." Cumber's face crinkled again, but more seriously. "All done in, y'say?"

Honus said: "Maybe you could tell me something, Mr. Cumber—"

"Sho, lad. You wanta know what ole Isaac Q. be doing way out here?"

"Well, sir, it does seem strange. I've told you why we're following the river to Reunion. But taking a large wagon over this rough country when there's a good road to the south is something else. And—you're not going our way, or we'd have cut your tracks. You're moving west."

"That I be."

"Hardly need to point out that you're heading into Indian country—alone."

Cumber's slaty eyes slitted. "Oh, the redskin's got nought

against ole Isaac Q. Ain't never touched the fuzz on my scalp yet. Y'see, I'm the post trader at Reunion. Like to leave my ole woman in charge and get off away from things now and agin, prospect a mite. Wagon is a sight of trouble some places I go, but I likes to travel in good style. All the comforts o' home. 'Nother reason too. Lemme show y'all—"

Cumber got to his feet and motioned them to follow him. Stepping around to the rear of his wagon, he undid the thongs that secured the puckered flap. Honus peered inside. He saw a few prospectors' tools, enough grub and gear for a long stay in the wilds. Also a pile of such goods as blankets, bolts of trade calico, mirrors, hatchets, knives, salt, sugar and tobacco.

"You can't need all this for yourself," Honus said.

"Places I go, you 'most always run into Injuns. Lone families, usual; sizable band oncet in a while. They's friendly 'nough they see you got a good rifle and a handy eye. Even so, fair idea to stay on their good side." Cumber waved a hand. "That's why this here stuff from my store."

He thrust his arm into the wagon bed and pulled out a chunkily bulging jutesack. He reached inside and handed Honus a piece of rough black ore full of jagged gold streaks.

"Don't aim for no big shuckins' with this gold-picking, but man knows the right places, he can 'most always scrape up enough to pay for his trouble. With me, it's fer the fun."

Honus juggled the chunk of ore in his palm. "It might not be worth a man's life, sir. You must have been aware that Spotted Wolf and his people are rampaging. . . ."

"Pshaw, young feller." Cumber held out the sack, and Honus dropped the chunk inside. "Traded with the Cheyenne plenty in kinder times. Always treated 'em straight. Spotted Wolf knows me from way back. 'Course I don't trade none with hostiles, but I ain't never been bothered by 'em neither."

"You may find all that's changed. They'll be wilder and bolder . . . with those new rifles."

Cumber patted his well-kept gun. "With Ole Henrietta, I c'n shoot rings around any Injun alive. Never saw ary redskin could shoot worth a bucket of buffler chips. Heh heh. Ain't none ever gonna get close as he needs to pick off this ole bull bear."

As he talked, Cumber kept studying Cresta Lee with his smooth gray-pebble eyes. "Ain't I seen you somewheres, young lady?"

"I doubt it."

"Well, there's a caution." His face screwed up into that living corrugated map. "Can't give over a notion I seen you. Say you got a young man at Reunion?"

"Yes; Lieutenant McNair. But this is my first visit to Reunion."

"That so. Know Johnny McNair. Dandy young officer. Lord declare, I'm a-clacking on like a likkered squaw. How you two been eating?"

"Berries," Honus said, almost apologetically. "I don't shoot too well."

"That so. Well, I was about to rustle up a jack for supper. Didn't count on two exter mouths, but mebbe c'n bag two. Don't like to dig into the grub I brought along till need be. No saying how long I be out here."

"Mr. Cumber," Cresta Lee said brusquely, "I'm wondering if you might supply me with some of that cloth. Also thread, needles and shears. This dress is all but falling apart. And my shoes . . ."

"Sho, Missy. Always tote plenty sewing stuff for the squaws. Keep the girls happy, you keep the boys happy. Heh heh. Got a pair of exter moccasins you c'n have. You wait a bit."

He climbed into the wagon and soon emerged with the desired articles, including a bolt of calico with bright broad stripes of red, yellow and black.

"Be back directly with them jacks. Soap's in my rucksack by the fire. You folks clean up, do whatever you've a mind."

Cumber winked bawdily, cackled and padded away through the trees, rifle swinging in his fist. He headed downstream at an easy lope.

Cresta Lee rolled out the colorful bolt and, kneeling beside it, began cutting a piece to suit. Honus, disagreeably aware of his accumulated grime and sweat, decided to avail himself· of Cumber's suggestion.

He found the lump of lyesoap in the trader's rucksack and left the camp, crossing the wooded angle of riverbend to its other side. By now the sunset had rimmed the west hills like a bloody halo. Standing in the rank brush, he stripped down and entered the water. The stream was fairly wide and deep here, the water clear and cooling. Honus scrubbed his hide to the hue of a fireman's eye and mulled over the presence of Isaac Q. Cumber, Reunion sutler (if such he was), many miles from the fort and pushing on alone into the wild plains north of the Janroe.

Maybe he was only what he seemed. A frontier eccentric with a touch of gold fever. His wagon contained only a few non-sinister trade goods. But he had known Cresta Lee—or thought he had. Interesting . . .

Honus left the water, shook himself as dry as he could, donned his dirty clothes and returned to camp.

Cresta Lee had quickly fashioned a curious but ingenious garment from the strip she had clipped off the calico bolt. She had cut a hole in the center, poked her head through so that the cloth draped her back and front, poncho-like, to the knees. Folding the material over in broad pleats, she had sewed these with a few quick stitches, then taken in the remaining slack by cinching her beaded Indian belt around her waist.

Honus sat down on his haunches and cleared his throat. "How is it that Cumber thought he knew you?"

She had discarded her shoes, which had burst apart at the soles and were held together by ravelings from her dress. Now she was trying on the moccasins Cumber had given her. She didn't bother to glance up.

"How the hell would I know?"

"Well, he seemed to think he'd seen you. . . ."

"For instance where?"

"Maybe in Spotted Wolf's camp."

It was a random shot, and it drew the coldest of stares from

59

her. "Try not to be more of a fool than you can help," she said in her meanest tone yet.

The moccasins were a surprisingly good fit. Cumber had small feet. Satisfied, she removed them, then peeled off the remnants of her stockings. Her fine legs were smooth and tawny. Honus looked away, discomfited. Though it made little difference—the stockings had been reduced to ravels anyhow.

She rolled the remains of stockings and shoes together and tossed them into the bushes. Then she picked up the moccasins and got to her feet, saying, "The way you usually stare, a leg or two shouldn't embarrass you. Limb. Pardon me."

Honus felt an agonized heat pour into his face. "That's not true. I mean . . . I never stared."

"That is to laugh. In just a couple of days, you've damned near looked a hole through me."

"I have not!"

"Bull," Miss Lee said quietly. "You through with the soap?"

He handed it to her and carefully did not look as she walked off behind the trees.

The bath had eased away the worst of his aches, turned his drugged fatigue to a pleasant lassitude. Honus stretched out on the grass, his fingers laced behind his head.

From downriver came the crack of Cumber's rifle. He hoped the trader had bagged a rabbit . . . and could get one or two more. Honus' mouth watered at the thought.

He tried to ignore the noise of Cresta Lee's lusty splashing beyond the trees. Had he really been looking at her that way? And what did she expect if she was going to waggle along in front of men all the time?

But he had to allow a grain of truth in her charge. Anyhow the minor proprieties seemed pretty silly out in the middle of the plains. Honus came from a long line of people who had believed that the sight of a woman's stockinged ankle was enough to topple whole citadels of righteousness and unleash maelstroms of sin. Ridiculous, he thought. For two days he had followed Cresta Lee's compact little figure in that disintegrating dress, and his self-control was perfect.

She came back to the clearing, a perky and pleasing sight in her bright new poncho-dress. She had thrown away the drab tatters of the old dress too. The gaudily striped calico marvelously set off her sturdy milkmaid's ripeness, her bare golden arms. She sat down on the grass and began fluffing out the thick dark ropes of her wet hair. Her skin had a clean lovely glow.

The bath must have done wonders for her spirits too: "Look, I expect I ought to thank you."

"What for?"

"For saving my life, that's all. When that Cheyenne was chasing me."

That had been two afternoons ago. And she was thanking him! Honus let his eyes droop shut. "Quite all right."

His coolness touched her temper again. "Listen, that makes a debt and it'll be paid. I've never owed anyone a damned thing in this life, and I never mean to. Understand me, Buster?"

Honus didn't answer.

After a strained moment, she said very quietly, "Now look. I'm sorry about your friends . . . all those troopers. I really am."

He opened his eyes. She was sitting with her knees drawn up, not looking at him.

"You might have said so before now."

"I didn't know how. Maybe I still don't. It's just . . ." She scowled pensively at her hands clasping her knees. "Death doesn't mean the same to everyone. You have to understand. I grew up on the East Side of New York . . . with my dad till I was eight, then in an orphanage. But it was all in one big slum. People died all the time. They died in ways I can't describe. Then I was with the Cheyenne these two years. That was a lot worse. Do you have any idea what white men's diseases do to those people? A little fever that'd make your ears hum can lay them out—kill them."

She gave him the blue-lightning jolt of her glance. "So don't expect me to feel about dying the way you do. The way your kind of people does, I mean. Because I can't. I've lived around death all my life. It gets to where one thing matters. Keeping alive yourself."

Honus was jarred by the revelation of her slum childhood. He wondered what he should say.

"Thanks," he began lamely. "'Hem. Guess that was pretty hard to say."

"Well . . . oh, bull." She seemed embarrassed. "Look—"

Cumber's rifle made another clear smacking report.

Cresta Lee looked at him quickly. She lowered her voice. "Uh . . . listen. What I said, you know, about this Cumber fellow? Not seeing him before? Well, I did see him . . . twice. In Spotted Wolf's camp."

"Yes," Honus said woodenly.

"What do you mean," she said ominously, "by 'yes'? You say it like it stood to reason I was lying."

"Well, weren't you?"

"What's that got to do with it! Look, Little Boy Blue, I want to make a new life for myself, if I can. I want to start by forgetting all about Spotted Wolf and his damned tribe. Maybe people'll have the ordinary decency not to throw it up to me. At least I can hope. Does that make sense to you?"

"But don't you see that this is important? If he lied about trading with the hostiles—"

"Well, what of it? Last time I saw him in their camp was months ago, long time before they ever got these rifles. I never saw him trade 'em anything but blankets, mirrors, the sort of things you saw in his wagon. And did you see *one* rifle in that stuff? Did you?"

"No," Honus admitted.

"Well, there you are, for God's sake! Will you stop all this piddling and prying? My God, I'm sorry I told you anything."

Honus gazed moodily at the wagon. An idea hit him. He got up and walked toward the vehicle, intending to take a closer look inside that back pucker.

A movement to the side of the clearing caught his glance. Isaac Q. Cumber had stepped from the trees in complete silence. He stood there like a gaunt uncrouching ape and watched Honus progress across the clearing.

Honus' stride didn't falter. With aplomb he angled past the rear of the wagon box and stepped around to the water keg lashed to the vehicle's opposite side. A gourd dipper was attached by a thong to the keg. Honus raised the lid and scooped up the clear water and drank, then nodded at the two jackrabbits in Cumber's left hand.

"See you had luck."

"Yeh." Cumber's bland pebbly eyes did not move off Honus' face. "Purt' fair."

He tossed the rabbits to the ground. Both had been shot squarely through their heads.

Chapter Eight

One way or another, Honus thought, he was going to have a close look at the inside of that wagon.

But his chances of sneaking a look seemed slim. After his successful hunt, Cumber remained close to the camp. He quickly and expertly skinned the two gutted rabbits and seared them, and the three of them took turns at revolving the spitted carcasses on a green stick laid across two crotched sticks over the low coals.

The well-grilled meat was delicious, but Honus' appetite was mechanical (if voracious). All he could think of was that expression on Cumber's face when the trader had surprised him heading for the wagon.

The idea that the wagon might hide more than harmless trade goods—for it was a large and heavy vehicle to carry just those few articles plus a camping outfit—had been an idle one. But no more. Not after that look of Cumber's. Honus knew he was downwind of something touchy. *Rifles?*

Cumber had lied about his dealings with Spotted Wolf, according to Cresta Lee. That might be understandable, for even if he'd delivered only innocent goods to the hostiles, the Army frowned on citizens who trade with those whom the U.S. government held itself unofficially at war. But for Cumber to head into the heart of wild plains country to pursue a hobby of gold hunting while Spotted Wolf posed an increasing threat to all whites—old friends or not—had a thin ring to it.

Something else, too. Nearly all of Spotted Wolf's warriors were now armed with the new repeating Winchesters. But he was rapidly building up his band. In a month it might be doubled. And with it his need for rifles.

So a second shipment at this time would be in order—with payment promised on delivery.

Probably it had begun with what Cresta Lee had seen: a petty illicit trade with the hostiles. Then Spotted Wolf's need for good rifles had suggested bigger business. Much bigger.

It would mean a lot of trouble and a considerable risk even to a professional trader, to arrange a secret inlet for those guns. And twice the trouble and danger for him to convey the guns out from his storehouse under the Army's nose, to a rendezvous far on the plains.

But easily worth it to get his hands on the small fortune in that paymaster's chest. (That, Honus guessed, would be the gunrunner's own idea for payment. And who outside of the fort commandants would know more about a paymaster's coming and going—when he might be expected where, the number of his escort troops and how they were armed—than the fort's sutler?)

Cumber was quite chatty through the meal and afterward. If anything, he got friendlier by the minute. A natural reaction, Honus reflected, if he wanted to put even a fleck of suspicion to rest.

The trader did not appear to be watching either of them carefully, though Honus guessed that he was. More than once he caught a casual puzzlement in Cumber's face as he glanced at Cresta Lee.

What if he remembered where he had seen her? Anyone who had seen Cumber in Spotted Wolf's camp could put him in deep trouble. Worse than that if and when the authorities began to look for someone on whom to peg the gunrunning.

If he recognized Cresta, or if he thought she or Honus suspected anything, it could be all up with them. But Honus had already decided there was more at stake here than their lives.

"Been right fine having some'un to talk with," Cumber said toothily, though he had done nearly all the talking. "Come morning, I'll give you young folks another big jackrabbit feed and make up a sack o' grub fer you to take 'long. Ought to get you through to Reunion in prime shape."

Honus thanked him. Miss Lee spoke of payment.

"No need, heh heh, no need. Y'all get some sleep."

Honus lay on a trade blanket spread near the crumbling fire. He stared at a cobalt sky frosted with starlight, restless with his suspicions and feeling a gnawing need to get at the truth even if he had to put a gun on Cumber.

He hesitated—he wasn't sure of Cumber. But all the more reason to make sure.

If he made a move, could he count on Cresta Lee's help? Most likely, feeling as she did, she'd take Cumber's part. But was that fair? For one minute before the minute had collapsed in the usual snappish row, he had found a break of humanity in her.

He almost smiled. She was a very tough and very bitter girl, but she had dropped her guard enough to let him glimpse a warmth that could be reached. *Only how do you reach it again?*

Oddly that was his last thought before he dropped off. Not of Cumber. Not of the rifles. But of Cresta Lee's small angry face finding a gentle moment. . . .

A slight noise woke Honus.

He had gone to sleep with his fist around his drawn revolver, which he held tucked between his right leg and the blanket. Sudden as his waking was, he had the presence of mind not to move.

False dawn muffled the plains like a pale gray pelt. The air was clear and cool, and true dawn wasn't a half-hour away. But what had aroused him?

There it was again . . . a leathery creaking. He saw Cumber ease out through the back pucker of his wagon and drop to the ground. He was fully dressed, carrying his rifle. He stole from camp like a shadow now, vanishing in the trees.

Nothing particularly suspicious there. The trader had unrolled his soogans inside his wagon last night. An early riser like most plainsmen, he was going out to fetch in the promised rabbit breakfast.

Honus threw his blankets aside and rose and skirted the dead ashes of the fire. He stopped by Cresta Lee's blanketed form, reached down to shake her awake. Her eyes opened—dark and cold and suspicious.

"What d'you want?"

"Cumber just left camp, I guess to hunt. This is my chance. I'm going through his wagon."

She broke off a yawn and raised on her elbows. "You're what!"

"I think Cumber's the one that's selling Spotted Wolf his rifles. I think there are more of the same hidden in that wagon . . . somehow. I'm going to find them, and I'll need your help."

Honus told her his reasons briefly. Her eyes seemed darkly to digest his words as if they weren't arguable. But she said flatly: "If you think I'm setting my head on a block for you, you're crazy. Suppose he's doing what you say? What business is it of yours? Or mine?"

"It's my business," Honus said grimly, "when some greedy bummer gets my troop butchered so he can get his fingers in a money chest. My business when he sells the Cheyennes guns that will be used to renew a bloodbath that finally got settled. Dull Knife's been threatening to break reservation, come north. All right. He'll watch to see how Spotted Wolf fares . . . and that will do it."

He paused to isolate his next words—they held a softly distinct warning. "Before you say anything at all—don't say 'bull.' Just don't."

"I wasn't going to," she said in a sullen mutter. "But I don't see begging trouble now. All we do is notify the commandant at Reunion. That'll settle him—if he's guilty."

"Not good enough. We're miles from the fort. By the time we've warned the Army and they've sent a detachment after Cumber, these rifles'll be in Spotted Wolf's hands."

"You're doing some tall guessing, Buster. If you're wrong—"

"I'll apologize," Honus snapped. "We've just been lucky so far that he couldn't place where he saw you before. Are you going to help? Or have you lived with the Indians too long?"

The slow dawn showed a quiet color rising in her face. "I'll help. But copper your bets before you move. Did it occur to you that Cumber may have left just now to test us?"

"It occurred. That's why I'll need your help. Here—" Honus thrust his Army Colt into her hand. "I want you to get off in those bushes on the west side of this clearing. He knows a few Indian tricks, but so do you. If you see any sign of him—if he tries sneaking up . . ." Honus hesitated, then tapped the pistol. "You'll have to use it. Don't take any chances."

Cresta Lee shook away her blanket and stood up, her dark cool eyes watching his face. "He's a dead shot—remember those rabbits? I'd be lucky to hit a barn broadside."

"We've no choice. Our two lives against a lot of lives—if any more guns get into Spotted Wolf's hands. Hurry up. He could be back any minute."

She crossed the clearing and slipped into the undergrowth. Carrying his Springfield, Honus walked to the wagon now, leaned the rifle against a rear wheel, and swung himself up through the pucker.

Kneeling in the wagon bed, he struck a match. The sulphurous flare of light washed back the sickly gloom under the canvas. Honus ran his fingers over the planks, trying to locate any sort of a panel. He opened his pocketknife and inserted the blade here and there and pried, but the boards were tongue-and-grooved beautifully together.

After a moment's thought, he climbed out of the wagon and inspected the endboards and sideboards carefully. No doubt about it. On every side, there was a uniform difference of three inches between the outside and inside depths of the wagon box.

He was sure now of a hidden compartment in the bottom. But where was the door?

The underside of the wagon—that had to be it! The least likely place to look. A trapdoor perhaps—or more likely a sliding board that would have to be neither raised nor lowered. . . .

Honus slid under the wagon. Ran his hands over the bottom boards, pressing up, sideways, forward, back. Nothing. He tried to jam his knifeblade between the board joinings, but as with those above, they grooved solidly together.

Baffled, Honus crawled out and stood up, slapping both palms against the wagon box. He felt mad enough to rip at it with his hands. He let his frustration boil back to a simmer. And did some thinking.

Suppose there was no door at all? That boards were removed to expose the compartment—and nailed back? But all the planks inside and out were so grooved together that none could be removed without splintering the edges. Any fresh break would show.

As he framed the objection, the answer came.

Honus gripped the rear endboard with both hands, testing it. He glanced around at the pink growing dawn, worrying about the noise he would make. No help for it.

He gave a strong yank. Nails shrieked. The whole board ripped away, exposing a flat narrow space between the two layers of planks. He could see only a row of rifles' buttplates, which was enough.

Cumber cackled quietly.

"You getting an eyeful there, sojer boy?"

Honus melted to the ground and rolled between the two back wheels. He dropped on his belly behind the right wheel and reached around it for his rifle.

The mellow roar of Cumber's Sharps devastated the silence. A tearing flash of pain in his cheek—Honus yelped. His hand flew to his jaw and a hot trickle of blood.

His Springfield lay only inches from his face now, mechanism smashed and the stock split. A flying splinter had hit him in the face. He lay shaken, unmoving, his eyes traveling the line of brush. He saw a whitish haze of powdersmoke, but nothing else; he guessed that Cresta Lee hadn't, either. She was wisely keeping still, waiting.

Honus thought he could pinpoint where Cumber was, but when the trader spoke again—softly chuckling—his voice came from a different place.

"You was acting kinda peculiar last night, younker. Figured to give you all the rope a man could want. . . ."

Honus heard the Sharps being cocked. It boomed again. A numbing blow on Honus' left foot: his boot heel flew off as if ejected by a powerful spring.

Cumber cackled some more. Ice congealed around Honus' guts. Was the man crazy? Did he intend—?

"You across the way—Missy!" the trader called suddenly. "I know you're hid up in there. You hyper out now and throw away that hogleg."

No answer.

"Missy," Cumber yelled, "you best—"

The Colt banged sharply.

Cumber's chortle was followed by a faint rustle of bushes, as if he were changing position again. Cresta fired a second time.

Cumber roared happily. He sent a bullet into the dirt close to Honus' outflung arm. The flinty earth spewed against his burned palm, which was still tender. He jerked the hand back. He bit his lip to keep from yelling.

"Miss Lee!" He let the pain go in a strangled shout. "Stay where you are! Don't mind—"

Cumber's next shot flung dirt straight into his face. It filled his mouth. He choked and spat, and was half-blinded.

"Now you hear me, Missy—" Cumber deliberately cocked the Sharps: a wicked cold-metal sound with a promise of death in it. "You come out. Square in sight, no tricks, and lea' me see you throw that gun away. Or the next 'un goes square between his eyes. You got that?"

"Yes."

Cresta Lee spoke quietly. Honus rubbed his knuckles against his eyes, trying to clear them. The sun was redly cracking the horizon. Leaves rustled. She stepped out of the bushes, the Colt held over her head.

Honus gasped: "Don't."

She looked at him. Her face was drained of all expression. She tossed the gun to the ground.

Cumber emerged from the foliage, a squat and primal shape in the streaming light. His eyes were like hot steel chips. He kept chuckling, his rifle raised, ready.

Honus scrambled from under the wagon and climbed to his feet. A nerve was jumping in his torn cheek; it made his eyes water so that he could hardly see Cresta Lee.

"You're a very funny girl," he told her. "You've been so tough. And you turn soft at the wrong time."

She was watching Cumber as he came toward them. She said nothing.

"Don't you see," Honus said bitterly, "that if you'd stayed hidden, there was a chance . . . a chance you'd have gotten him? That all you've done is postpone it for me—for both of us?"

Cresta Lee glanced at him. Her eyes seethed with anger. "Yes, you damned fool—I do see it."

Chapter Nine

After putting away a good solid breakfast, Cumber crouched on the creekbank and scoured his frypan and plate clean with water and a few handfuls of sand. His prisoners sat by the dying fire with their knees drawn up, hands and feet bound with rawhide thongs. He hadn't bothered to feed them and neither would ask him to.

With his appetite satisfied, the trader had turned garrulous again.

"Knowed I seen the little lady some'eres, but couldn't peg it for a good while. Come to me just before I dropped off last night. Seen her in Spotted Wolf's camp that coupla times, she was gussied up like a squaw, all the doodads, even her hair. That's what throwed me off."

He cackled pleasantly.

"I only been sutlering at Reunion a year. Knowed McNair all right, and rec'lected hearing his young lady was carried off by Cheyenne a coupla year back. Cinched it all together. You run off, hey? Sure be a caution to see ole Spotted Wolf's face when he claps eyes on you."

Cresta refused to twitch an eyelash. Honus strained his wrists apart with all his strength. The thongs bit painfully; he desisted.

"Plumb waste, boy. She's cured leather." Cumber said it

cheerfully, not even appearing to look his way. "You two was pretty much an accident for me, y'know? Ordinary, I foller the river 'stead of the road. Don't meet up with a living soul thataway. Not that I go sneaking off the post or nothing. Can't hide a big wagon should anyone come a-looking for it. What I do, I allus keep some gold pretties handy. Dust, a few egg nuggets, that poke full o' ore chunks you seen. Show 'em about to folks around the post and brag up my pickings a little. Never show enough to tempt anyone to foller and dust me off fer my poke. Just enough to make 'em figger I'm a shade dotty from gold fever. Throws off the lot."

His gray-glossed eyes snapped across to Honus. "All 'cept fer you. And you wasn't nigh as smart as you thought, was you, boy?"

"I guess not."

"Hah! You bet your tintype not. Or you wouldn't be trussed up for no Cheyenne basting."

He had a fine literal way of putting things, Honus thought dourly. In fact the idea of delivering them into Spotted Wolf's hands seemed to tickle the trader no end. When it would be easiest all around to just knock the two of them in the head and leave them.

Honus said so.

"Easy as falling off a log," Cumber agreed cheerily. "But you two's a handy insurance for coppering my investment, y'might say. See, I put in time and sweat a-plenty to set up this business o' mine with Spotted Wolf. Effen you're white, you don't just go riding into that feller's camp and allow you want heap big trade. There's Injuns come in off the prairie all the time to trade at my post—you can lay your eyeteeth they ain't all busted bronchos. Me, I allus spot the warriors, the bad bronchos, in a minute. I'd give away a blanket here, bottle o' whiskey there. Even a good rifle now 'n' then. Got to be knowed as a real *heves enevo*, good friend to the Cheyenne. Finally got myself took to meet the big Wolf hisself. Even then it was touch 'n' go a spell, I tell you. Lucky I c'n speak most Cheyenne di'lect pretty fair, make fast sign talk for what I can't spell out. Deal was cinched, but I don't trust that cinch none. Oh, Spotted Wolf, I reckon his word's plenty good. . . ."

"It is," Cresta Lee said quietly. "To any man. In your case, even to a maggot."

Cumber chortled mildly. "Spunky little chit, ain't you? Only thing, I ain't nowise sure about his braves. I been gifting his women right along, calico and beads and truck like that. Ladies think a sight o' me. Call me *veho pavhetan*. Good white man. But the bucks, they like as not skin me soon's they lay their red hands on this last batch o' guns."

"They won't need you then," Honus said. "But you'll need them. Isn't that it?"

"How you mean, boy?"

"The Army payroll chest. Your payment for the guns. Once it's in your hands, you'll be a target for every Army patrol. Unless you stay with the Cheyenne. Unless they help you reach Mexico or wherever. I'd say you'll need them, all right."

Cumber scratched his whiskers, his eyes faintly baleful. "Lord declare. Said you was a smart 'un, didn't I? All right. Cheyenne fighting man, he don't answer to no one, even no chief, saying he takes a notion to. They cotton to my scalp, even Spotted Wolf won't stop 'em. But now suppose'n I hand over the guns and the pair o' you, same time? They'll feel a sight more kindly toward old Isaac Q., leastways for a spell. Time they get feeling rambunctious again, I'll have something else figgered."

Honus could almost dredge up a fleck of admiration for the renegade: he rode his luck on a hair-fine edge. His aplomb was so perfect, you had a feeling that, no matter what, he'd make it out with his skin intact.

Honus had no such optimistic view concerning his own future. Or Cresta's.

Though it lasted only a day, the interlude that followed covered what were easily the most miserable hours of Honus' young life.

Cumber loosened the ropes on their ankles to let them climb into the wagon. Afterward he tied them again and pulled down the flaps on the front and back puckers. Then he hitched up his mules, climbed to the seat, hoorawed the team into motion.

That was where hell began for the two people inside. Began and stretched out like a nightmarish infinity. The rack. The boot. Those jolly Renaissance folk and their predecessors had been pikers, Honus thought.

Sprawled in the gray gloom, they were jolted and gouged across the splintery boards like sacks of inanimate meal over every bump and dip (at least one per foot) found by the jouncing wheels on the irregular prairie sod.

As the day wore on, it grew hotter. Under the tight-flapped canvas, it was like a young inferno. Sweat poured off them, soaking their clothes; they simmered in their own juices while they were sweated inexorably dry. Their rawhide bonds were so tight as almost to cut off all circulation.

By noon, Honus doubted that his angular frame could boast a single square inch of unbruised flesh. His fingers and toes felt dead and useless. He was dizzy with hunger, his belly forming one big growling cavernous ache halfway down. The only blessing he could count was that with his mouth and throat a tortured baking tunnel of awful thirst, neither bruises nor empty belly counted for too much.

Cumber made a midday halt. They knew it was midday because when he undid the front flap and stuck his elfin grinning face through the pucker, the sun slanted so steeply that the entire contents of the wagon stayed in shadow.

"Comfy?" Cumber asked.

Cresta Lee had a ready answer for him.

Even Honus, who had seen enough of her temper to expect almost anything, was taken aback by her choice of language. Cumber blinked, his jaw dropping in surprise. He sprang from the wagon seat to the ground and moved off, wondering in a *sotto voce* mutter what in the name of Tophet things were coming to, Lord declare, young woman talking thataway.

The sunlight and fresh warm breeze swept a small relief into the sweltering wagon box. And the jouncing had ended for a while. Thank God for that.

Otherwise there was less than nothing to exult about. Cumber built his fire and began cooking his bacon and coffee, whose aroma brought a surge of saliva to Honus' mouth and wound up his growling guts in a hundred knots.

He groaned.

"Listen—"

Cresta Lee had been twisting quietly around at his back, working close to him. Now she startled him by hissing in his ear.

"He can't see us now. Let's don't waste the time."

"What?"

"Pull yourself toward the back a foot or so. I can roll enough to reach your wrists then. But quiet and easy about it, for God's sake. . . ."

Honus complied, alternately jackknifing and straightening his body in small jerks, heaving his weight across the wagon bed by cautious degrees. This gave Cresta, who had been cramped against some heaped blankets, enough leeway to roll completely over and place her back to his.

He felt her fingers hunt for and find the hard knot on his thongs. The fumbling and tugging lasted for a minute. Then her angry despairing whisper: "No good. A body could work at these damned things a week of Sundays. And get nowhere in this damned position. . . ."

"Teeth," Honus managed to croak.

"That's it." A note of excitement cracked her discouraged, dry-husked murmur. "Make a little more room, Buster. I'll—"

"You stay like you are." Honus, in no mood for arguing, let the words out in a soft parched snarl. "My jaws are stronger."

He felt her stiffen instinctively: letting anyone else take the initiative was about as familiar to Cresta Lee as ladylike talk would be. But her realism conquered—as always. She remained obediently still while he maneuvered awkwardly around until, getting his face close to her wrists, he was able to get at the ropes. Toothwise.

By "cured," Cumber must have meant only that the rawhide was no longer green. It was also far from resilient. The thongs had the flinty iron-hard texture of a whetstone; Cumber had yanked them so tight that Honus had a hell of a time fixing his teeth around a couple of loops. And then he wasn't quite sure how to proceed. Did you go about gnawing through strips of rawhide by biting, grinding or sawing at 'em?

He settled for a stab at every method. Working up enough spit to soften the stiff leather some and almost gagging on the grease he produced.

He seemed to be denting the evil-tasting cords a little. The maddening need for haste lent a sweaty goad to his efforts.

An unbearable ache was settling into Honus' jaw muscles when, hearing Cumber grunt to his feet and kick dirt on the fire, he hastily quit his task and rolled away from the girl.

In a minute or so the trader had climbed back to the wagon seat. He gave them an idle glance through the pucker as he dumped his skillet, coffeepot and rucksack back in the wagon bed. Then he secured the flap again, yelled at the team, started the wagon moving ponderously forward.

Cresta tried to whisper something. Her words were lost in the creaking jolts of the heavy swaying vehicle. Finally she rolled over to face Honus and started to say it again. The wagon's sudden lurch banged their heads together.

Miss Lee's pretty mouth formed a ripe, silent, predictable oath.

Glaring into Honus' eyes from about three inches away, she hissed belligerently, "Well?"

"Not very much. That rawhide's tough. And there just wasn't time."

"All right—" She said a low furious expletive as another bump flung them hard together. "Suppose you keep trying."

"But—"

"Look, the flap's shut, isn't it? He can't see us! You might's well try."

He did. It was hopeless. Trying to close his teeth over the thongs again, he was flung this way and that across the lurching

77

wagon bed. He had to twist into an excruciating posture that made it impossible to hold his body steady. All he collected for his pains was, finally, another jagged sliver when a bump plowed his face along the rough boards.

When you weren't trying to chew the thongs off somebody's wrists, you were able at least partially to brace your body by wedging your back against one thing, your boots against something else. It ameliorated the hell out of a painful situation. Honus at last gave up and did just that.

"Son of a bitch!" Cresta Lee muttered.

He guessed that she was directing the nicety against conditions in general and not him in particular. At least he supposed so.

Of course the afternoon stint of spine-hammering jolts and suffocating heat was far worse than the morning one had been. It grew even hotter, for one thing. For another, the country was getting progressively rougher. The careening wagon box was on an almost continual stern-down slant that indicated they were gradually climbing.

By this, Honus knew that Cumber's route had swung from west to almost due north. The Platte country began to tilt toward higher ground at its north extremities. At least he could fix in his mind a rough notion of their direction. He and Cresta would need some sort of orientation, however crude, if they managed an escape.

Cumber would have to make night stop before long. Maybe that would offer the chance. Probably their last.

How near or far were they from Cumber's point of rendezvous with the Cheyenne? No way of telling. One thing for sure. Once in Spotted Wolf's hands, they would stand no chance at all. . . .

The fawn-colored light glowing through the worn canvas above them was turning to a rich pumpkin hue. Almost sunset. Twilight soon. He'd have to stop then . . . wouldn't he?

The wagon seemed to hesitate. Cumber cracked his whip with a savage hoorawing. The mules spurted into their harness, shuffled and danced, settled their weights for a solid pull. The wagon creaked and crashed up the early slant of a sharp acclivity. Iron clanked on flint as the wheel rims arched over big boulders, heaving the wagon this way, then that. Honus and Cresta Lee were tumbled back and forth, slammed repeatedly against pieces of rough-edged gear, against the sideboards and each other.

What had appeared to be a large flour keg was knocked on its side and sent rolling. It smashed Honus in the shoulder, then pitched on to crash against the tailboard.

Honus bit down on a yell of pure agony: his eyes watered with the excruciating force of the blow.

He twisted his head, peering. No wonder that keg had seemed weighted like an equivalent of solid stone. Two staves had shattered, spilling out a cascade of brass-jacketed shells that winked dully in the gloom. Of course. Ammunition for those Winchesters. Plenty of it. A twin of the first keg was nestled intact in a front corner.

They rocked up and over the hill, down its far side. At last Cumber reined in the team. Opening the fore flap now, he climbed into the wagon bed, saying cheerily, "All out—stretch your legs," as he took out his Bowie knife and with two deft slashes relieved them of their leg thongs.

Spotting the broken keg, he swore a little, then prodded his captives to their feet with his rifle, herded them to the back flap and ripped it open. "Jump down, little lady. . . ."

Cresta dropped to the ground. Cumber swung his arm. His calloused palm whacked Honus squarely between the shoulder blades, knocked him over the tailboard and sent him sprawling to the ground.

Cumber was convulsed with delight for a full minute. "Lord declare, Lord declare—"

Finally, wiping the tears from his eyes, he began tossing out grub, cooking utensils and his bedroll. Climbing down, he nudged his prisoners ungently over by a large lichen-mottled boulder, forced them on their backs and tied their feet again.

Honus had a bad moment or two wondering if Cumber

would check the ropes on their wrists now. He didn't. He moved off whistling and began to scrape up brush.

There was a good deal of dead stuff at the bottom of this deep swale, as if it had once cupped moisture but was now as bone-dry as the surrounding plains. Hills rose on every side of them, carpeted with the soft gold of short-curling buffalo grass. Memories of magenta and lemon stained the western rim of land, sucking the last brassy wash of daylight after it, the rich blue cowl of evening sliding down now.

Honus was not an appreciative audience. He sagged his back against the boulder, battered sore, his knees pulled nearly to his chest. He could not see his wrists, but he could guess at their torn, blood-raw condition after a day of rawhide; all the feeling was gone from his hands. At least his legs were protected by boots, as Cresta's were by the ankle-high moccasins, from the bite of thongs. But he was weak, his head swimming, from a day of baking and sweating out his body water.

Should he ask Cumber? No. Damned if he would. The trader was well aware of what dehydrating torture he'd put them through. He'd provide water as he would food—if and when it damned well suited him. He'd know that they must have food and drink soon, or pass out on him.

When he had his camp gear laid out and a light smokeless fire going, Cumber picked up his rifle and light-footed over to them, grinning pixieishly.

"You young folks gonna be almighty pleased to hear your misery's nigh done with. Figger to reach rendezvous with old Spotted Wolf 'fore noon tomorrow. You c'n start worrying 'bout that." Cackle. "Seen some fresh sign a spell back. 'Less I'm mistook, they ought to be some young pronghorn close to. Got a hankering for a juicy rump steak. Want y'all should have a filling last feed, too." Cackle. "Gonna scout acrost that rise yonder. May be a spell finding 'un to dust off. Gives you young folks a while to spoon some, say them last sweet nothings, whatever. 'Y God, don't never say ole Isaac Q. ain't overflowing with pluperfect-pure heart."

Cresta Lee had a fairly pungent opinion as to that. She offered it.

Cumber gave a rapturous roar of glee and moved away, rifle swinging in his hand. He went up the long north rise in swift bouncy strides and disappeared over the top.

"Quick"—Cresta Lee rolled her back to him—"get at these ropes! Hurry up!"

"I think," Honus mumbled around a thickly swollen tongue, "we'd better wait a little—"

"Wait!"

"Couldn't *he* be waiting—just over the hill out of sight, to see if we try something—"

"He *could* do all kinds of things, dammit! I'm concerned with how many minutes it'll take to get shed of these damn ropes! You get to 'em *now*, d'you hear?"

She was probably right. Anyway he was too keyed-up himself to wait even one minute. He dropped on his side and fastened his teeth gingerly around the thongs.

Minutes dragged by. Each one was an aching eternity of dogged, remorseless effort. He could no longer work up saliva of any description. He just chewed. And chewed.

His gums were sore and bleeding from the constant grinding pressure. Darts of pain shot up his jaws to where they hinged. The blood began to roar in his ears. He couldn't pause. Fighting more than a hardness of thongs. Time. Man's oldest nemesis. His worst. And always his last.

He couldn't keep this up much longer either. The muscles of his jaws were going slowly, achingly flaccid from the strain. But he could taste the increasing rough fray of the rawhide as the flinty fibers gave under steady punishment. He isolated one of the loops and worked at that one alone.

It parted.

"There—" The words left him in a raw, choking grunt. "Pull. Pull!"

Then it was Cresta Lee's turn to make an agonizing effort, jerking her wrists in opposite directions, twisting them up and down and sideways. Slowly she was working the slack of the broken loop into the neighboring turns of rawhide.

Another loop slackened. Dropped free. Another. She yanked one hand upward again and again. Suddenly it pulled loose.

Her wrists were lacerated savagely, streaming blood. But her hands were free.

Chapter Ten

Honus Gant was not only consciously unheroic—even his daydreams were modest—he had never remotely contemplated suicide, martyrdom or similar fates of the nervy. All things considered, it would be perfectly natural if, having made his sturdy attempt to throw a wrench in Cumber's plans and having only succeeded in landing himself and Cresta Lee in hot water, he now decided to abandon further efforts in that direction. And settled for getting the hell away while the getting was good.

In fact the thought distinctly crossed his mind. And lasted for about five seconds.

Cumber had been careless about retying their feet. Cresta had the knots on hers undone in about a half minute. Then she struggled to her feet and moved on quivering legs to the wagon. She rummaged under the seat where she'd seen Cumber cache Honus' revolver and their knives.

Coming back, she cut him free.

"Come on, Buster! We'll need food and water and guns. Let's get started."

Honus felt the blood gush back to his hands and feet in hot prickles. Bracing both palms against the ground, he shoved up carefully to his haunches, then onto his feet. His gangling frame rocked off balance the first few steps.

"Come on, Ichabod!" snapped Cresta Lee.

"All right! All right—"

They began swiftly ransacking the wagon for what they'd need. Some grub, a couple of blankets, matches, Honus' battered canteen, Cumber's own too. His rifle having been smashed by Cumber's bullet, Honus removed the tailboard that hid the rifle cache and appropriated a Winchester, then stuffed his pockets with .45-.70 ammunition. They slaked their burning thirsts at the water keg lashed to the wagon's side, and Honus filled the canteens. In all, these preparations took less than five minutes.

Cresta Lee, shouldering the rucksack of food, wheeled impatiently away toward the southeast slope. "Come on, hurry it up . . . oh no!"

She came to a dead halt, staring over her shoulder. Honus had plunged into a thicket. He was breaking off and gathering up the long tangled wands of dry brush in handfuls. He carried an armload back to the wagon and threw it between the rear wheels.

"For God's *sake*, Buster! Are you completely crazy?"

"Listen," Honus said doggedly, "all we have to do—"

"*All we have to do is get out of here!*"

"—is pile some of this dead stuff under the wagon and set it afire. The boards are dry as punk. Once it's got started, nothing'll stop it—"

He was already on the trot, still stumbling a little, toward another clump of dead brush. Cresta Lee said something that sounded opprobrious, but which eluded his vocabulary, then threw down her rucksack and pitched in too.

Honus guessed that his companion had reached the short end of altruism a good while ago, but with her usual sterling sense (seeing that he was determined) wouldn't withhold help that would enable them to be away that much sooner.

Another couple of minutes, no more, and they had the space between wagon box and ground crammed with dry brush. Honus went to the fire and picked up two blazing sticks, while Cresta, holding the Winchester, nervously watched the summit over which Cumber had disappeared. The indigo twilight was deepening quickly: if Cumber had had no luck, he'd be on his way back soon.

Honus pushed the sticks into the brush at opposite sides of the wagon. Stepping back, he watched the flames lap up in bright tumbling tongues, taking slowly at first.

"All *right*, Buster!"

She strode back to the rucksack, slung it to her shoulder and began an angry, slogging ascent of the south slope.

Honus made sure the flames had a good start, then grabbed up the canteens and blankets and hurried after her. Overtaking her about a third of the way up the hill, he took the rifle from her and then stayed close behind her as they climbed.

He didn't look back till they'd reached the top. By now the flames were licking up the sides of the box. They caught with a leaping flare at the old canvas. It peeled away in a sudden sheet of wrinkling ash and a dusting of sparks. Honus grinned. Cresta Lee tugged at his arm.

Cumber let out a wrathful yell.

He'd appeared quite abruptly on the rim of hill directly across the swale from them. He yelled again. And came plunging down the long lumpy hillside toward the wagon. The ruddy spout of fanning light lit him weirdly in his run: he looked like a squat dark troll sprung from some medieval woodcut, bounding down over the rocks.

Honus half-raised his rifle, but gave up the notion almost as it came. Running, the trader made an uncertain target in an uncertain dance of light. If he missed (as almost surely he would) he would draw Cumber's fire at once. For the moment, Cumber's whole concern was for his precious cargo.

Honus said, "Go on," and was close behind Cresta as they went over the crown of the hill and down its outer slope. They were cut off from Cumber. But maybe not for long. It depended on whether the trader would be enraged enough to try a pursuit.

If he did, he'd have a temporary edge. The country below them was open; he was deadly with a rifle. On the other hand, the twilight was thickening fast: in minutes it would fuzz into a mouse-colored dusk.

If they could lose Cumber then, all his tracker's skill (which Honus guessed was considerable) would avail him nothing. Till daylight. By then, after traveling all night, they would have put many miles between themselves and him.

They came off the long off-tapering base of the hill at a run. Ahead, a long darkening sweep of buffalo grass, lightly feathered by a coasting cool breeze. The whole terrain was almost black with twilight: blacker for the still-bright contrast of the vaulting sky, which gave the farthest undulating ridges a cameo-edged sharpness.

Honus ran swiftly behind the girl, accommodating his great lunging grasshopper strides to her dainty fleet-footed run. His heartbeats burned in his veins. Dusk—how far away?

Everything ahead of them was obscure, but he could feel the ground tending faintly downward as he ran, then felt a sparse lacing of taller grass whipping at his boots. A seep or something sent up a lot of ground moisture here, turning the grass rank and luxuriant.

Honus darted backward looks. Smoke from the burning wagon crawled skyward like a furling strand of sheer black silk —at first. Then it belched up in rolling smudgy clouds, belly-tinted a soft copper where the last streaky daylight burnished them.

The ammunition began to explode, chattering the silent creamy air into silken shreds, sounding like troops caught in a surprise small-arms engagement beyond the hill.

The vegetation increased under Honus' choppy strides. Yes —woody shrubs dotting the grass. Now, ahead, a belt of low irregular thickets, broken here and there by a gleam of water where no water should be—a spring-fed rivulet. A fringe of willow and chokecherry that shot out crabbed tangles of greenery in every direction.

Cover! They were—

A bullet whipped through the leaves. After it came the boom of Cumber's rifle.

Honus scrambled as deeply as he could in his run, twisting one more glance backward. Cumber on the hill, a dark oddly enlarged form against the fading sky. His high fierce yell. The light was bad, but there was enough to fix a running quarry to his plainsman's eye.

Enough to—?

Honus felt a clubbing blow in his right thigh. So hard that it numbed his whole leg even as it crossed his boots in mid-stride.

He tripped and somersaulted in the air, barreled completely off the ground by his own impetus. He lit with a jarring impact on his shoulder and side. Slammed over on his chest, he felt brittle grass-blades saw the flesh of his cheek.

He lay that way momentarily, thick-brained and unmoving in the narcosis of bullet shock and a stunning fall. Then he felt Cresta Lee close, kneeling, her hands pulling at him, her voice low and swearing and urging.

He managed somehow to drag the one leg up, letting his knee take his weight. Then he hauled up the other leg, aware of its curious numbness.

That was when the pain hit. A red superhot barb of pain that quivered like a thousand fishhooks shot through the back-to-front muscles of his thigh.

He started a yell, and half-gagged himself cramming its keening swell back into his throat.

"Shut up. Get your feet under you. Lean on me—"

Honus responded like an automaton. He clamped an arm around her shoulders. Head down, dizzy and stumbling, he fixed every atom of his will on stiffening the muscles of his good leg to take the full swing of his weight at each step.

They were moving into the thicker brush. He knew that from the scrape of branches along his legs and body. Hard to see. The woolly flood of dusk had blurred everything. Shot around and through now by a red throbbing darkness that existed only for him. . . .

"Down."

Cresta's insistent whisper. He realized they had come to a stop, she braced and leaning to take his whole weight.

"Down, *dammit!*"

He obeyed, letting his body sink against the strong tug of her hands. Damp earth against his back. Brush patterns pinwheeling blackly on the sky. Darkly, her head and shoulders bending. Her whisper.

"This'll do it . . . he can't see us now. Too dark. And we're far enough in the brush, I think . . . but he's coming. So be quiet."

He felt her hands relax and leave him, and her body shift a little away from him.

A spasm of pain hit his leg and rocketed into his groin. His eyes shut in his twisting face: his neck tendons strained like cables. He fought not to cry out. A squeaky groan trickled from his lips.

Cresta hissed gently. Her fingers found his wrist, closed, clamped tight.

He heard a thrashing in the bushes. As if Cumber were slashing at the foliage with his rifle. The sounds grew closer, they receded, grew close again.

The trader seemed to be zigzagging through the heavy growth, blindly aimless in his anger, beating savagely left and right. Muttering continually, and finally inarticulate in his rage.

Cresta Lee sat motionless, bolt upright beside Honus. Light glinted softly on the barrel of the Winchester held between her hands at a muzzle-up angle. He hoped to God that she wouldn't take the chance—in this near-darkness and being the execrable shot that she was—of trying to pot Cumber.

That possibility may have occurred to Cumber. At least he abandoned the search after no more than a few minutes. Or so it seemed to Honus. Then he was moving away; the noises diminished.

"Gone now," Cresta Lee murmured. "How bad?"

"Bad enough, I guess. But I can walk."

"Sure, but how far?"

Her tone was soft and wry and bitter. He guessed why: until

now, he'd represented a small security to her mind. Now, suddenly, hurt and needing help, he was a dangerous liability, a threat to her safety.

"Go on," he said hoarsely. "Get away while you can. You want to, don't you?"

"Oh, don't be a fool."

"You're the fool. The debt's paid. Go on."

"What debt?"

"One you mentioned. For saving your life. I figure you paid that when you threw away the gun this morning . . . to keep me from getting shot."

"Well, what the hell, Buster! You've got yourself shot *anyway*, haven't you?"

"That's now. I'm talking about earlier. Debt's paid. Nothing owing. All debts canceled—"

"Will you *shut up* about that damned debt?" Cresta Lee let the words out between her teeth. "Here . . . let me see that leg."

She pulled her sheath knife and ripped open his pants leg, before and behind. By now the whole leg was soaked with blood, and Honus could feel it puddling in his boot.

The bone wasn't touched. That was all he was sure of, and thankful for that much. But it was deep and bad, and he wondered—as she had—how far he'd get on such a leg . . . even with her help.

Cresta hacked off a piece of one blanket to make a tight hasty bandage around his thigh. She cut off another strip to make a crude sling for the Winchester, another for the blanket-roll itself, the rucksack of grub stuffed inside it. She slung the rifle and canteen and bulky bundle across her shoulders and stood up.

"Give me your arm. Now sit up as I pull. That's it, boy. Now. . . ."

She grasped his arm with both hands, braced her legs and leaned her weight backward. Honus inched from his seat to a shaky, wobble-kneed stance. Cresta dropped his arm around her shoulder and again grabbed him firmly around the waist.

"Now *try* to help me all you can, Buster. You're a big boy and I'm a little girl, remember? I know you can't put much weight on that leg, but keep it straight and use it to steady yourself as much as you can. I don't like to push, but we have to get as far the hell away as we can before morning."

"Cumber?" Honus said in a muzzy whisper. "Will he bother with us now? . . ."

"How do I know? He hasn't a damn thing to lose, has he? Doubt he'll go on to meet the Cheyenne now. The same moment they learn that load of guns got burned up, his fuzzy scalp won't be worth a nickel. What's that leave him? Just wringing our necks. Come first daylight, when our trail's plain . . ."

The night hours crawled by in a weary and kaleidoscopic agony. Honus' senses frayed off on a slow tide of rising fever. Still Cresta Lee dragged him on, on. How far, across what kind of country, he never knew. . . .

Odd splinters of impression riddled his brain. Starlight flung like a vast frosty blanket across the prairie. His vague awareness that his stumbling, shambling gait was slowing them desperately. The crying need to rest . . . lie down . . . sleep.

But they kept on while the night lasted and the sky turned a weary gray. Till it seemed that he had never known anything but the spurt of tearing pain and the nerve-scream of exhaustion.

These things and Cresta Lee's sturdy shoulder, her strong arm, attached him to reality. And these too ribboned finally, fragmentarily, off. A roaring pit of fever yawned under him and he was falling, falling forever. . . .

Chapter Eleven

It was shortly after first light when Cresta came on the cave. Not really a cave either. Really an upslanting burrow that was a sight too low and narrow to move about in with any comfort.

It was formed by a mammoth chunk of sandstone that must have rested for ages in a tilted position on the hillside till enough earth around its base had eroded away to let the big slab tip and fall. Now it lay on its flat side some yards below its original bed, toppled in such a way as completely to cover a deep-gouged arroyo under it. The hollow thus formed was blocked at its upper end; a wide low opening was left below.

Cresta had been keeping a careful eye out for something like it. Any sort of shelter that would keep off the weather and serve to hide herself and a wounded man.

She had dragged the stumbling, semiconscious Honus for God knew how many miles through the interminable hours while darkness held. Using the stars to hold a southeasterly route that she hoped would bring them back to Janroe River.

She was nearly dead with fatigue. Her arms and legs were livid with scratches from the forests of brush she had fought through. She hadn't had a bite of food in thirty-six hours, and her whole body was one vast sore-muscled ache.

Cresta was by no means soft. Her long captivity had taught

her whatever a deprived childhood hadn't about hard work and bare survival. But she couldn't remember feeling this spent, full of a weariness that ate into every nerve.

By the time the mousy drab of false dawn had broken to a few tabby-colored streaks in the east, she was still going on a woolly thread of sheer will and a pure stubbornness dredged up from some deep reservoir that she hadn't suspected in herself.

By now she was ready to drop. And almost did. Then the increasing fan of dawnlight began to rim in harsh relief a range of tall rocky hills ahead. A sight that infused her with a slight hope. *Maybe!*

All night long she'd been leaving a plain trail. She'd had no choice. With Honus in tow, she was unable to take the precautions that might have thrown off a tracker of Cumber's probable caliber.

If she were right, Cumber would be on their trail as soon as it was light enough. And following the blundering route they had left through thickets and tall grama grass, he would come fast.

These rocky hills might be the answer. If she could throw him off here . . .

She struggled on, pulling Honus with her. He was nearly insensible, mumbling with fever. He fell repeatedly. Each time she managed to slap him back to his feet.

At the edge of the hills, she left him and scouted around, careful to walk only on rocks or heavy gravel, which were plentiful. She found a clear stream of water. And she found the little cave.

After beating it for snakes and other tenants, she packed Honus back to it, guiding him over the rocky path she had picked out. She noted each place where his clumsy driving stride scraped furrows in the gravel or where he flicked off a drop of blood.

She dragged him into the narrow hole, tugging him by the wrists. Then went back and painstakingly restored each pebble of disturbed gravel as it had been, burying those which bore spots of ruby wetness. Collecting dead loose tangles of brush, she piled them by the cave mouth. She'd use these to cover it, but not yet. She needed light enough to examine his wound.

A glorious sunrise was flooding the hills by now, pouring nicely into the tunnel. When she'd untied the blood-crusted bandage, it looked about as bad as she had expected. Inflamed around the edges and bleeding freely.

He'd lost too damned much blood already. Constant exertion had kept it pumping out.

She cleaned the wound with water from the canteen and cut more strips from the blanket to tie it up again. That would have to do for now. She knew of several herbs that the Cheyenne used. Later she'd see if any grew hereabout.

Right now she had to concentrate on Cumber. Stay where she was and wait for his coming. Or wait long enough to make sure he would not come—whichever.

She made Honus as comfortable as she could on the blankets. His face was flushed and sweating; he twitched in his sleep (if you could call it that) and mumbled, his eyes squeezed shut as if he were seeing things behind them.

What was it with him, she wondered, watching his face as she munched a biscuit and a handful of jerky. She'd never met anyone quite like this farmboy-schoolmaster-soldier.

He had a fitting sense of irony or poetic realism that she wouldn't have suspected if she hadn't heard him quote those lines over his dead friends. Poetry, not biblical either.

Wry intelligence, then. Even sophistication of outlook now and then, blending peculiarly with a pure yokelism.

For Honus Gant had done the incredible: he'd managed, somehow, to retain into his mid-twenties a kind of boyish innocence that would have been surprising even in a man of far less intelligence.

That innocence was, she supposed, the mainstay of his idealism. She had never understood idealists. All she knew about them was that a genuine idealist (outside of a fool) was a rare bird.

Maybe that was what made an ordinary man like Honus

stand out. For rare or not, he was ordinary—with his dreams of a little farm back in Ohio. Like any brainy man, he must have other, better dreams too. Yet that one satisfied him.

And he certainly wasn't heroic—not in the accepted sense. He was plainly ill at ease as a man of daring, of action—yet he was willing to take chances that only a crazy man or a very brave man would. And probably for no better reason than that he was just doing a job he believed somebody had to do. How much, she wondered, of real idealism was no more than that?

"*Dammit!*" she said aloud, quite irritated with herself.

She picked up the Winchester and got to her feet, bending over deeply, for the burrow wasn't above four feet high at any point. She moved back to the entrance, sat down on the cool crumbled earth, crossed her legs tailor-fashion, and watched the new day grow.

She had a good vantage from here. The cave pierced into the hillside about halfway up. The hills rose vastly all around. But a man approaching wouldn't come over them, clambering across those monolithic litters of rock. He'd come through one of the saddles between them, also rugged going but the easiest way. That gave her only three likely approaches to watch.

The whole thing was, what would she do if and when?

If she were a halfway decent shot, she damned well knew what. But she wasn't. The rifle would have to be a last resort. What she had to do was keep still, watch and wait—and hope.

Some of the irritation ran out of her. She knew what was really bothering her. It was that some of her actions lately hadn't made much sense, even to her. Examined in the light of her brittle creed, they just were not reasonable.

Well, what the *hell!* She couldn't have very well deserted a man she was owing to, could she? On reflection, though, that reason, taken by itself, stood on a shaky underpinning. She was, after all, putting her own neck in jeopardy with such loyalty. The idea of leaving him *had* flickered across her mind —just after he was hit. A reflex of the moment, a natural one. Maybe it had made her feel guilty enough to stick by him no matter what. Hell! That made no sense either.

She felt puzzled. A little uneasy. And gave it up.

The sun scaled higher. The rocky floor was getting warm. She pulled the brush she had collected across the mouth to block the hot rays, arranging it in such a way that her vantage wasn't impaired. Then she crawled back to look at Honus.

He was a little quieter, but the fever was fixing all its red-hot claws in him now. His face was puffy and lobster-red; his skin was burning up. His leg was swelling too, enough to strain the bandage against the drum-tight flesh. The bleeding had stopped.

She took up her post again. She had two enemies now. The one she was watching for, and the one already surrounding her, unstoppable and merciless. That was exhaustion. A numb suffocating deadness of body and spirit that became harder to fight off as the drowsy warmth of midday came on.

Cresta kept pinching herself awake and rubbing her painfully swollen and scabbed wrists where the rawhide had scraped them raw. Her shoulders were sorely chafed from the carrying straps of the gear she had toted all night while supporting a wounded man. She couldn't risk sleep as yet, but she dared a small hope now. Cumber would come soon. Or not at all.

None of her aches or pains seemed enough to hold off the crushing tiredness. She felt it to her marrow. The dead monotonous glare of sunpoints on rocks was maddening. She kept muffling yawns. Heat shimmered in veils off the bare slope. Her eyelids felt crusted and heavy.

She maneuvered her back against a jagged spire projecting from the wall. It hurt like hell. But it worked. It kept her awake. . . .

She jerked alertly up on her haunches.

Something was moving down in the sun-blasted rocks where the far left saddle began. She watched tensely. Cumber stepped into view.

He was moving along at his usual rolling tireless lope, his rifle cradled in both arms. His head turned restlessly, conning every foot of the terrain, his face in black shadow under the flat crush of his hat.

He'd followed their plainly marked trail quite easily. Would he also spot her camouflaged one? What about the brush covering the hole: would it look natural to an observer down below? She held the Winchester lightly across her thighs, watching. *Go easy,* she told herself.

Cumber had come to a halt, peering slowly about. She smiled. He was baffled, no doubt of it. Now he was turning his face to the upper hills, sweeping everything. No sign that he discerned anything amiss.

She guessed his next step would be to start hunting around. How far would he carry his search? That was the question. Hidden or not, this cavern could be spotted from close up.

Suddenly Honus let out a dry heavy groan.

Oh for God's sake!

She twisted around to look at him. He groaned again, louder. He began to struggle up on one elbow, his eyes opaquely varnished with fever. He started to babble, a string of incoherencies that ended in a grating muffled yell.

Cresta was already scrambling on her hands and knees to reach him. She slapped a palm over his mouth. "Shut up, dammit! You'll have him up here in—"

His delirium turned to violence. He fought, and she couldn't hold him. His big-knuckled hand swept out in a blind backswing, slamming her in the temple and knocking her away.

Cresta rolled sideways, closing her hand over a fist-sized piece of rock. She surged to her knees as Honus came up on both elbows, his mouth opening wide.

He never got out the yell or whatever. Cresta simply clipped the rock around and clouted him in the head. He went limp.

She crept back to the entrance and seized up the rifle. *Oh Lordy. That did it.*

Cumber had started forward again, moving at his slow yard-eating lope toward the base of their hill.

In that moment she was sure Honus had given them away. Then she saw Cumber stop again, his head slightly cocked. And he was looking off right, not upward. Cresta delicately eased the rifle butt to her shoulder and dropped the sights to his chest.

Don't let him come closer. I'll have to. And I'll miss for sure. Dammit! Johnny told me something once about shooting downhill. Don't even remember. . . .

If she was forced to shoot, her only chance was to wait . . . wait until he was so close that . . .

Suddenly he started up the slope. Her pulse jarred. But he was coming at an angle, not toward them. He halted and poked at some rocks, and she clearly heard him swear. Then he prowled away and finally passed out of sight across the curve of the hill.

Cresta waited for what seemed a long time.

At last Cumber appeared again, stamping over the rocks. A gaunt anger stiffened his ape-bowed shoulders and rolling legs. He headed back straight for the saddle. He'd lost the trail and his quarry might be miles from here.

When he had gone, Cresta sagged down on her side, pressing her cheek to the cool rock. With the off-drain of tension, her weariness was like a vast fist pressing her to the earth, the cool earth and sleep.

Fighting it, she dragged herself back to Honus.

She had soaked him pretty hard. Split his scalp, in fact. The blood oozed richly dark against the carroty blaze of his thick hair. She washed the cut with the last of the canteen water, then ripped off some more blanket.

She wasn't sure of Cumber. He was as sly as they came. It might be a grand act; he could always circle back. Well, if he did, he was due for a disappointment. She wasn't moving a step from this nice cool cave until she had slept.

Not for too long, she thought drowsily, curling up on the cool rock. Just for a month or so. . . .

She woke in the last velvety glow before sunset. She yawned, stretched and checked on Honus. He seemed to be no worse for the blow. It was all fever now, making him sweat more than ever and jerk fitfully in his sleep.

She picked up the two canteens and clambered down the

slope. Maroon shadows stretched behind the rocks. She went to the little stream and rinsed out the canteens and filled them. Then she prowled around the hills awhile, studying the scant vegetation.

She was in luck.·

She recognized a tall stubby-leaved weed with yellow star-flowers. She didn't know what it was called, but she'd seen the Cheyenne women make a poultice of incredible efficacy from its root. After digging up the gnarled roots, she returned to the cave.

She unbandaged and washed the swollen leg. The frontal wound, where the slug had emerged, was by far the worse. She didn't like the look of it one bit. It was the sort of wound for which a surgeon might recommend amputation.

Well, that was out of the question. She'd have to do her best by what was available. She made the poultice as she had seen the Cheyenne women do, chewing pieces of the root to a black pulpy mess on which she almost gagged, then rubbing it into the wound.

Afterward she made a light supper off more biscuit and jerky and filled the slack in her stomach with water. At least she needn't skimp on that. The grub would stretch for two, maybe three weeks if she pared her diet back to the bare subsistence level to which lean times with the tribe had accustomed her, and supplemented it with roots, bark, berries and the like.

And stretch it she'd have to. They could be stuck here a long time. No matter which way it went with Honus now, she faced a battle for his life that would go nip and tuck.

With the die cast, though, she felt calm. No misgivings. Her philosophy was governed by practicality, not sentiment. If you could, change things for the better. If not, make the best of 'em.

Honus kept her awake most of that night with his groaning and bellowing. She hoped to hell that there were no hostile ears within better than a mile radius, for his ravings would fetch them sure. She changed the poultice every few hours, dribbled a little water in his mouth now and then, and had hell's own time trying to hold him down.

By morning his leg had ballooned to nearly twice its normal size.

He slept part of the day, tossing constantly. Cresta went down the hill once, to refill the canteen, gather some more roots and wash out the blood-caked bandages. She couldn't afford to discard a one; cloth was too dear. While digging up the roots, she made another pleasant discovery. Shoots of wild licorice growing in luxuriance. She cut a good supply of them, chewing some as she walked back to the cave.

The leg was festering indescribably as to sight and odor. Twice in his delirium he tore the bandages off and started the holes bleeding again. All she could do was change poultices, rebandage, keep the flies brushed away. And another weary day passed into another horrendous night.

The crisis was near. The appearance of his leg made her sure of it. She thought that the drawing strength of her poultices had confined the infection. If so, the leg could be saved. But the thigh, puffed with poisonous juices, resembled a discolored and misshapen keg. She knew what she'd have to do.

Toward morning she bared and cleaned the thigh, then heated her knifeblade, slowly turning it in a small fire at the cave mouth.

Returning to Honus, she knelt, for a moment watching his face, the skin pale yellow under a fiery scrub of whiskers. His eyes were squeezed shut in his hot shining face, his head moving loosely.

She poised the blade over his thigh and plunged it deep into the swollen flesh. Ignoring his shrieks, she deliberately widened the cut. The foul-smelling fluids gushed out. She kneaded the flesh with a fierce strength; he was too weak to fight her now.

The night was quite cool. The muggy heat had lifted and there wasn't a fly about. She left the wound open to drain.

By morning, his fever had gone down. So had the swelling. She poulticed and bandaged. While she worked on him, Honus slept on like a man drugged. Healthy, healing sleep. . . .

99

Chapter Twelve

First of all, as he opened his eyes, Honus saw flickers of bright orange against the blackness. His vision steadied a little. The flickers slid into focus: a fire.

What had actually awakened him was the sound of somebody cussing. Familiarly.

Cresta Lee, he saw, was crouched in the tunnel's mouth, nursing a finger she had apparently burned while feeding sticks into a small blaze. This was set barely inside the entrance so that the smoke would funnel out into the night.

Honus started to raise his head. The stabbing pain in his head, a roar of nausea in his belly and ears, made him change his mind. He brought one hand to the raw throbbing ache at the top of his head and felt the lightly scabbed flesh. It burned like fire. His mouth felt like an oven. He croaked for water.

Cresta Lee brought one of the canteens over, lifted his head a little and gave him some. "How's the leg?"

He looked at her blankly. "The leg?" He tried to move his legs. One stirred a little. The other wore a bulky weight of bandaging. It really hurt like hell. He chuckled feebly. "Thought it was all in my head at first."

"You got hit with a rock," she said succinctly. "Rather, I

hit you. Cumber was looking for us and you started getting loud. So I put you out again."

"Cumber?"

"For God's sake, Buster! Don't you remember?"

He did. Some of it. He remembered breasting the endless singing waves of pain and fever. And always a girl's face—this girl's—close at hand sometimes, at other times seeming to float away, but always drawing close again. Things were pulling back together in his mind like a sluggish patchwork.

"How—long . . . ?"

"We've been here? Just three days." Her tone implied what a nuisance it had all been. "Want another drink?"

The water was cold and pure. "Where did you get it?" he husked.

"There's a little stream down below. Spring-fed, I guess. Easy on it."

His head was a little clearer. "Is a fire safe?"

"What do *you* think? But it was turning cold and you're still a sick boy. I've kept it small, and piled up some brush just beyond the mouth—shelters it pretty well."

"And you've stayed by me all this time?"

"No." She eyed him with a fine distaste. "Whatever gave you that idea? I'm a mirage, didn't you know? I'm a hundred miles away, Ichabod, and you made me up. That's the honest-to-God truth."

Honus flushed. "I didn't mean that. But if I had . . . well, you've done your best to convince me that if it *did* come to your neck or mine . . ."

"Haven't I just," she said coolly. "You'll never know, Ichabod, because it never came to any such choice."

"Didn't it?"

"Oh, for—" An angry vein pulsed in her throat as she started to her feet, bumping her head on the rock ceiling. "—God's sake!" Bent over, she rubbed her head and swore tenderly. "Would you do me a favor? Go to hell back to sleep."

She returned to the fire, knelt and began breaking up small

sticks to keep the flames stoked at a constant level. The firelight polished her flesh rosily.

He tried not to watch her. As she was in his line of vision, though, and he could hardly move his head, it was hard not to look. The striped poncho-dress, stained now, dirty, laced with brush-tears, revealed pretty near as much as it hid. The tattered knee-length skirt made no secret of her strong full legs, golden-smooth, lovely in the firelight.

She didn't seem to pay him any attention. But after awhile she said: "Getting a little overwrought, aren't you, Buster? I mean, a man in your shape . . ."

Honus felt himself redden to the roots of his hair. "I wasn't —I mean, it's—it's becoming, that's all."

"*What* is?"

"Your dress," he whispered weakly.

"Oh, for—! The *dress!* This thing! You damned well *know* what's in your eye."

"All right," Honus said resentfully. "But to hear you, you'd think that's all a man ever thinks about—where women are concerned. . . ."

Miss Lee gave a soft hoot. "And what else, pray?"

"Well . . ." God, how did he get into these verbal impasses? "There are other things . . . er, higher things."

"Above the legs, you mean? Please—don't give me that lofty, superior tone of yours."

"I'm not—"

"The hell you're not. You've been looking down that damned long cornbelt nose of yours at me since we met." She had turned on her heels till she was facing him, and he saw the undisguised hostility in her stare. "You haven't the simple manhood to come out and say it, have you? I was an Indian's woman. I belonged to an Indian. That's what gravels you, doesn't it?"

Honus blushed even more confusedly. "Why, I, uh, hadn't really thought about it."

"Like so much bull you haven't!" She came to her feet—with enough presence of mind this time to duck her head—and stood with those sturdy legs planted firmly, hands braced on her hips. "There's not a one of you that hasn't since the day I arrived at the agency. She's been had by an Indian—she's damaged goods! What would satisfy you? If I'd killed myself? Or died of sheer disgrace? Or if I'd been broken into a leathery ugly hag? Well, fellow, I did what I had to do to stay alive, and I'd do it again. You hear me?"

He blinked at her unhappily, trying to understand what it was she was suddenly so angry about. "Yes, of course."

She wasn't finished. "*Maybe*," she lashed him, "if I'd put on a jutesack, heh?—and heaped ashes on my head. Oh, *that* would suit you, if I were humble and contrite and properly debased. Then, by God, you and the rest of the good, good people could forgive me! Well, damn all your chinchy little souls!"

"Look!" Honus husked. He felt harried and exasperated. "I don't care one way or the other!"

"Oh, *don't* you! With everything else, my fiancé is an officer and gentleman, a true and gallant gentleman who is willing to take me back, sight unseen, no questions asked. How it must eat you all up that I needn't care one damned fig what you think—because I have a man who's too big to care."

"If he knows you, he probably wouldn't dare to," Honus muttered. "I wouldn't want to contest a breach of promise suit on Army pay either."

"Oh, you're so smart, aren't you?" Her eyes blazed darkly; she flung her head back in scorn. "What are you anyway? You're *nothing*. Johnny McNair is *twice* your size. And he's ten times as smart!—graduated at the top of his West Point class. And he's good-looking. And he—"

"—has money."

"You're damned right he has money! And he has real aspirations in life, not just a mouthful of smart crap that you could get out of any broken-down schoolteacher who can't set his sights on anything higher than grubbing out his days on a stinking dirt farm."

Honus swallowed. He was too sick and weak to afford the

luxury of an outburst, though he'd never desired more keenly to give vent to the submerged Gant temper.

"That being so," was all he could think of to say, "I don't see why you didn't marry him back East."

"And it's none of your business why either, Buster!"

"It seems to me," Honus said resentfully, "that you've done your best to shove your business down my throat. And I told you, didn't I, that I have a given name? There's no need to—"

"Why not?" Wicked glint in her eyes. "What's wrong with 'Buster'?"

"It has a derogatory sound, that's what! And that other name, Ichabod, I don't know, I think that's even more insulting."

Cresta Lee gave him a grin with sand in it. "Ichabod," she chanted. "Ichabod, Ichabod, Ichabod!"

After two days more, Honus was well on the way to recovery, though still weak. These poultices of hers were a miracle, he thought. First they had drawn the poisons and very probably saved his leg. A couple of more days of them and it was plain that they'd also quickened the healing. After that Cresta Lee abandoned poultices altogether and had him stay outside the cave for hours at a time, his leg open to the sun and a leafy branch in his hand for keeping flies away.

He'd thought that her sharp and unwarranted display of temper would signal a downturn in their relationship—and had braced himself. Surprisingly, it hadn't worked that way. Quite the contrary. Next morning she'd been more cheerful than he'd seen her. Placid—no. Whether Cresta Lee's moods were sweet or sour, she never shed that impudent toughness. She was a merciless tease, for one thing. But that was better than quarreling.

Having plenty of time on his hands, he thought it over. The answer wasn't hard to come by.

She was stuck fast in that tough, lonely posture of hers. She couldn't even admit to herself that she cared what other people thought. But she did care, she cared deeply. The wound in his leg was nothing to the one that had festered in her mind—

with people like Agent Long's wife and Captain Battles, rest him, to feed it. And the knowledge that there'd be dozens more like them to face. . . .

Then the constant exhaustions and tensions of these last few days, finally the strain of caring for him through three days and nights. All that her state of mind had needed was the trigger of his innocent remark.

Well, he didn't mind, Honus thought humbly. She had every right.

Anyway, getting it out of her system had brought about a few subtle changes between them. They could now talk about little things—nothing important—without generating friction. Even that little was an improvement.

In other respects, though, they were no more at ease with each other than they'd been from the first. Outwardly things were better; underneath he felt restless and snappish, and he suspected that she did too. Being stuck together under these circumstances wasn't helping any.

Honus had something else on his mind. He didn't know exactly how to approach it, but it had to be said and soon.

On the morning of their sixth day at the cave, he sat out in the sun, his back propped against a rock and his leg out straight before him, swishing at the flies. Cresta sat a few yards off, biting her underlip concentratedly as she repaired the tears in her dress with ravelings, using a splinter to "eye" them through tiny holes made with her knifetip.

"Dammit all to hell!"

She threw away the splinter, which she had run into her thumb. The outburst seemed perfectly natural.

Honus almost smiled at the thought, thinking how her swearing had annoyed him at first. She was no more profane, after all, than an ordinarily profane man. He was, he suspected, getting so that the next time he saw a girl shed a maidenly tear over some vexing trifle, it would seem ungenuine.

Less distracted by her body now, he'd gotten used to watching her face. He'd always been too agonizingly self-conscious with girls to look closely at their faces, he realized. And hers was an interesting one—sensuous, a little sad, faintly scornful even in repose. Her mouth was full and soft, with wide sensual lips that she usually held tomboyishly compressed. Her eyes were a richly dark concentrate of the sky's blue. Her body showed only a wonderful animal vitality—her face held a dozen things he could name. A hundred more that he couldn't.

She turned her head, sun racing across her glossy chestnut hair. "You do know how to flatter a girl, Mr. Gant."

"I was thinking," he said lamely, "about Cumber."

"Hoh! Yes you were."

"Look," Honus snapped. "I've been thinking this. How long before I'm in shape to hike clear to Fort Reunion? Weeks maybe?"

"A couple of weeks. Maybe sooner, depending on—"

"All right," he said impatiently. "That's no good. Cumber's had nearly a week to make it back to Reunion. With a story of how he lost his wagon—any story would do. Thing is, there's nothing to keep him from picking up again and getting more rifles—"

"Oh, pooh! He wouldn't dare. Knowing the two of us are alive. Huh-*uh*. He'll go to Reunion maybe . . . and just keep going from there."

Honus shook his head. "I don't think so." He shifted on the warm rock, feeling for a pebble that was gouging his buttock. "His payment from Spotted Wolf was to have been the small fortune in the paymaster's chest. That fellow has guts—and greed. If possible, he'll try to get his hands on more rifles and carry out the bargain. Take the chance that you and I are lost and starving, that we'll die out here." Moodily, he pegged the pebble at another rock. "Even if we don't, he'll know that with me wounded, he could easily beat us to the fort and still have time to make new arrangements. . . ."

"Hmp." Cresta examined her thumb, scowling at it. "Well, what of it? He's right, isn't he?"

"We don't know what his source of guns is, so we can't tell how long he'd be getting another shipment. A week? A month? My point is, we *can't* wait. The Army has to be notified of that fellow's activities just as quickly as we can get 'em the word."

Cresta Lee raised her eyebrows, then frowned them together. "Oh no. Oh no, Buster!"

"It's the only course that makes sense—"

"Yes, *nonsense*! Dammit, what d'you think I am? I know you don't give a peck of wormy goobers if you get us both killed trying to nail Cumber—you've proven that a couple times —but I have my code too! I'm not leaving you out in the middle of nowhere with a gimped-up leg, and you can't hit game for sour apples. So forget it."

"Now listen." Honus leaned forward, letting his good leg take the strain, his tone deadly serious. "Thanks to your treatment, I'm healing up fast. Well enough by now to shift for myself. Stretched fine, there's enough grub to last me two weeks anyway. There's a stream of good water, and I can make it down with the aid of a crutch—a staff. There's not a thing more you can do here."

"Oh, for God's sake."

"For the sake of a lot of innocent people, you've got to make Reunion as soon as you can. You can send help for me. What's important is—"

"Yes, I *know*, Buster."

She gave him that richly disgusted stare that he knew so well. Its essence was that she could be his or anyone's equal in damnfoolery. Also, and it might have been a trick of the sunlight, he thought he saw that faint-breaking warmth in her that he had seen once.

Cresta Lee sighed. "I do know. . . ."

Chapter Thirteen

There were only three. A man, a woman, a small boy. They had but two horses, one for the man to ride, the other to carry his wife and to drag the travois that bore the child and the family's few possessions. Their clothes were a mixture of Indian buckskin and white man's trade stroud; they belonged to no band and their people might have been any of the plains tribes.

"*Pave vona*," Cresta said. "*Heves enevo*." Good morning. I am a friend. She tapped her breast.

They had been making camp when she had spotted them and made a careful, open approach. They had promptly quit work and the man had picked up his rifle. Otherwise they made no move, their faces masked like bronze.

She couldn't tell whether they understood her or not. Well, all she knew was Cheyenne—with a smattering of the universal sign talk of the plains. It would have to do.

"I look for the white men's fort to the east," she told them, reinforcing her words with gestures. "Am I close to the little river that leads to it?"

The man gave her a dumb and sullen look.

Obviously he was wondering what in the name of Maheo or

somebody a lone white woman was doing on the deep plains where no white should be. Would she have friends nearby—perhaps waiting behind the hill over which she had come? No. Clearly this one—though she talked like an Indian—was lost. She was armed too, with a large revolver shoved through her beaded belt, her hand resting on it. Lost or not, she looked very confident, this white woman.

The boy plucked at his mother's buckskin skirt. *"Niva tato?"* His eyes were very bright. *"Niva tato?"* He was very insistent; who was the stranger?

"Hekotosz!" She slapped his hand away with a warning to be still.

"You are Cheyenne," Cresta said evenly, "and you know my words. *Eahata.* I ask again."

The man took his damned good time deciding to answer. He pointed. *"Mila hanska,"* he said roughly.

Cresta nodded, her face expressionless. *Mila hanska*—Long Knives. The Sioux-borrowed term for U. S. Cavalry. But he'd pointed definitely toward the northeast. Not the south and Janroe River. Nor toward the southwest where Fort Reunion lay.

Did he mean different Long Knives, she wondered—perhaps a detachment of pony soldiers in the field?

She put the question to him.

Yes. He had seen Long Knives on horses. No, not many. Perhaps five times the fingers of both his hands.

That seemed improbable, thought Cresta. The massacre of the paymaster's detail might well cause troops to be ordered out in force and into hostile country. But hundreds of them, not a patrol of fifty.

She plied him with more questions and learned that the Long Knives had been accompanied by two heavy wagons which kept them down to a snail's pace in this hilly, hummocky country.

Wagons?

Well, she'd never pretended to understand the ways of the

Army. At times they defied reason. It seemed nothing less than lunacy—after the fate of Captain Battles' detail—for the brass hats to send out so small a patrol into Spotted Wolf's country. But to burden them with two cumbersome vehicles to boot!

"*Etoneese?*" When had he seen them?

"*Onohetto.*" But a short time ago; less than a sun.

His black-pebble eyes glinted; his words were clipped, almost angry. Cresta guessed that he did not like whites, nor did he want trouble with the whites. He wanted her to be gone. Also he was not lying.

"*Zeo notaseas. Nataemhon.*" She raised her hand, palm out. I leave you now. Good hunting.

She moved off from them at a slight sidling angle, keeping her head turned enough to keep the family head and his carbine well inside the tail of her eye till a hillock cut him off. On the lonely plains, a good revolver might be reason enough to dust off a woman of the whitebellies.

Since leaving Honus yesterday morning, she had covered ground briskly, heading due southeast by the sun and keeping an eye ever peeled for the meandering line of greenery that, cutting darkly against the yellow swells and dips of sun-cured buffalo grass, would denote the Janroe's twisting course.

Once she was beyond the Indians' sight, she tugged the big service revolver from her belt and restored it to the rucksack slung across her shoulder. Grimacing, she rubbed her hip where the weapon had quickly gouged it sore. To carry it boldly for this meeting had seemed wisest. ("You keep the rifle," she'd told Honus. "The pistol's a hell of a lot lighter, and I can't hit anything 'less it's under my nose. Of course neither can you.") Other than the .45, the rucksack contained only a little jerky and bread. She had one of the canteens too. ("I don't need very much," she had assured him. "I can make do on roots, you know. And you're so damned finicky.")

She resumed her steady trek. But not in the original direction. After taking a careful bearing by the early sun, she changed her course by almost an acute angle. Now she was forging on a beeline toward the northeast.

If the Indians had encountered a patrol of Long Knives sometime late yesterday, then she was one hell of a lot nearer to them than she was to Fort Reunion. Reaching Janroe River would take her another half day anyhow, and she'd be a good four days in reaching the fort.

If not for the wagons, she wouldn't consider trying to overtake a mounted patrol. But with wagons, they'd be lucky to cover five or six miles in a single day, now that they had left the military road. She should find them before nightfall. A dispatch rider could take her news to Fort Reunion. And she'd lose no time in guiding a party back to Honus.

She was feeling more and more uneasy about leaving him alone at the cave. Suppose that something . . . a relapse . . . anything. The wound had seemed to be clean and healing nicely, but you could never be sure about gunshot wounds. Suppose that he were found by hostiles? She'd been taking careful note of the country she was crossing (and what few landmarks could be found on this bland and treeless terrain), but suppose that she were unable to find the cave again?

For God's sake! What are you, a brood hen? Stop clucking. His neck's at least as safe as yours is just now. . . .

By midmorning, she finally hit the trail of the patrol. It was as plain as broken grass-blades, hoof cuts on virgin prairie sod, fresh horse droppings and the twin slicing ribbons left by two heavy wagons could make it.

The patrol was heading north. She took up their trail at a steady swing. By midafternoon a tender ache was attacking the muscles of her calves. Her pace turned deliberate and slogging. Ordinarily she would have halted for a rest. But she was close now.

The sun had sloped deeply west, throwing out her shadow in a grotesque bobbing silhouette. Then she spotted the pale furls of smoke rising against the blue evening. Supper fires. Bivouac for the night.

She was still a weary two or three miles from them. Cresta

summoned up her last energies and didn't let herself think beyond one step at a time.

The camp was set well off from the hills, on a rolling yellow esplanade of plain. As she neared the bivouac, Cresta straightened her shoulders, making her walk strong and confident. Not hurrying either, but conscious of a quiet excitement. Men's voices shredded the soft air with talk, laughter. The familiar sight of troopers moving about accustomed duties was pleasant.

A detail of men was picketing the horses out beyond the wagon mules, nosebagging them. One man spotted her and nudged a companion. They all turned to stare. A man whistled. Another laughed.

Suppressing a grin, Cresta singled out a tall weed of a corporal who was almost goggle-eyed with astonishment. She halted about a yard from him, giving him a cool and appraising study that shook the poor jackanapes up even worse.

"Oh, soldier. Where's the officer in charge?"

"Arrrumfff—"

The corporal was too confused to fight words past a thick chew of plug cut. He settled for jabbing a thumb wildly toward his right.

"Thanks."

Cresta tossed it across her shoulder as she headed straight as a string across the camp toward the two big Studebaker wagons. As she passed the orderly rows of pup-halves, troopers broke off whatever they were doing to crane their heads and stare.

God, she must cut a splendid figure by now. Some regalia to cross a camp of men in. The once gaudy poncho-dress was reduced to tatters, discolored by sweat and filth and dried blood. Her hat was a dilapidated piece of straw matting. Her bare arms and legs were scratched and dirty. The beaded Indian belt and moccasins added a barbarous touch to the picture.

Cresta, however, was only mildly self-conscious under circumstances that would throw other women into tizzies of mor-

112

tification. What occupied nearly all her attention was the gut-knotting aroma of fresh coffee.

The two Studebakers were drawn up at the far side of the camp. They were ponderous affairs, painted Army-style: lead blue for the wagon boxes and Venetian red for the wheels, lending a look of solid garish masculinity. An officer stood by the front of one, talking to a sergeant. Barking at him, it sounded more like. But from the words Cresta caught, he was merely giving an order relative to the disposition of sentries.

The two saw Cresta at the same time.

The noncom's jaw dropped. The young officer seemed flung into total consternation. His eyes started out and his sun-boiled complexion surrendered to a darker red that flushed from his thick neck up to the line of his close-cropped pale hair.

He was speechless.

Cresta, noting the shoulder straps with two silver bars each, nodded crisply. "Lieutenant, my name's Cresta Marybelle Lee—"

"Cresta! Good Lord!"

She had taken a vague notice of the fact that another man was rummaging about inside the wagon. Suddenly he parted the front flaps, vaulted across the seat to the wheel and then dropped to the ground.

"Cresta!"

"Oh for God's sake! Johnny!"

Lieutenant John McNair caught her around the waist in a happy bearhug, whirled her off the ground and set her down. He grinned at her, unable to contain his happiness.

"Cresta!"

His face was pleasant and engaging, but somewhat short of handsome. He was rather slender of build, a little above medium height, but wiry and strong, as her near-bruised short ribs could testify. His eyes were dark and fine, sparkling with a moist happiness that made her feel almost guilty. She was glad to see him, but . . .

He kissed her, whirled her around and set her down again, and started to kiss her more thoroughly. Flustered then, he broke off and, holding her in the circle of his arm, turned to the other lieutenant.

"Er—Karl, my, uh, fiancée you've heard me mention. Miss Lee. Cresta, this is Karl von Leibnitz. . . ."

"Madam!"

Von Leibnitz snapped a salute, gave a stiff bow and clicked his heels together. All in one flow of stiff reflex. His face was still the hue of a turkey's wattles. He was stocky and muscular, about thirty, but acted like an uneasy hybrid of abashed boy and a soldierly caricature from a comic opera.

Happy times, Cresta thought. *A true oaf of oafs.*

She mentally braced herself before giving a pleasant nod and smile. "Not quite yet, Mr. von Leibnitz. Madam, that is. But thanks."

"Cresta!" McNair caught her by the elbows, devouring her with his eyes. "I can't believe it! I thought—I was sure that the Cheyennes had you again. When Battles' detail was found . . ."

"I got away, Johnny. But not alone. Listen, could I sit down? I'm about dead."

"Yes—yes! Sorry!" McNair picked up a crate that improvised for a camp stool and set it against a wagon wheel. "Closest thing to a chairback here. Now please, tell us—"

"Madam," said von Leibnitz. He seemed to have difficulty with his words. Beet-red, he harrumphed. "You had, I take it—ahem!—a mishap with your clothing?"

Cresta looked at him expressionlessly. *So that's what's bothering the poor lump.* "Several, Lieutenant. Several. Wouldn't happen to have an old soup sandwich about you, would you?"

McNair groaned and slapped his palm against his temple. "Good Lord, how thoughtless can a man be! I'm sorry, darling. I'll get my greatcoat. Karl, can't your striker fix something to eat right away?"

"Of course. My apologies also, Miss." Von Leibnitz bowed jerkily, then strode away, calling, "Robbins!"

McNair climbed into the wagon and emerged carrying a double-breasted military greatcoat with a sleeve-length cape.

"Here, darling—" He helped her into the vast garment. Cresta smiled at the way it reached to her toes.

Von Leibnitz returned with a chunky private who unhooked the wagon's tailgate and began pulling out pans and grub. Cresta composed herself on the crate and started to talk. The two officers sat on their heels and heard her out, exchanging amazed glances now and then. Occasionally one would interrupt with a question.

"Cumber," McNair muttered. "Rifles for Spotted Wolf! And smuggled into—and out of—the fort under our noses. Suppose he could've had them shipped in a case at a time and concealed under other supplies in his warehouse. . . ."

"It is fantastic, John!" Von Leibnitz shook his head. "Are you sure, Miss, that you did not dream some of what happened?"

McNair said gravely (giving Cresta a sidelong wink): "You wouldn't suggest that my fiancée is lying, would you, Karl?"

"No, no, you must not think this," von Leibnitz said hastily. "I mean that out on these plains, the sun gets very hot, and . . ."

"I'm crazy," Cresta said agreeably.

"No, no! I do not say this. I will send a man back to Fort Reunion at once, with a message for Colonel Tabler. It will tell him what you have told me—then he will decide what to do."

"What d'you mean?" Cresta frowned. "What's to decide? I told you what we both saw—Honus Gant and me."

"I suspect what Karl means," McNair put in, "is that this'll put the colonel in an awkward position. No doubt he'll detain Cumber—take whatever steps are necessary. But reluctantly. No commandant at any fort will interfere with the post trader by choice, Cresta. Naturally he has the authority. But the sutler's position is a political plum. The assignments are made in Washington, which means that the man who gets one has influence with some capital muckymuck—a senator likely, or a War Department brass hat. The more pull, the better his chance of getting a big post on which to set up business. And it's a lucrative business!"

"Yes," von Leibnitz nodded. "This is what I mean."

"Listen." Cresta's jaw began to harden. "I'll testify to what I saw. So will Honus Gant. And I'll testify that I saw Cumber twice in Spotted Wolf's camp. Drumming up trade with hostiles. How does that tie in with his alleged gold hunting?"

McNair smiled. "Easy—easy. I believe you. And you know I'll stand behind you, no matter how sticky it gets. As there's a good chance it will—very. We might have a fight on our hands, clear to the Capitol dome. Where, I might add, my dad has quite a few friends too. All right?"

"All right."

She grinned at him and shifted gingerly on the crate, trying not to be too obvious. The evening was warm and the great-coat's thick kersey was turning into a hot, scratchy, itching torment.

But it had to stay on, and no complaints either. Henceforth she'd have to think twice of behavior that might embarrass Johnny. He was a terribly resilient fellow (had to be, to swallow her), but even so . . .

"Listen, Lieutenant," she began, and paused. That was another thing: her abbreviated manlike directness. *Careful. Say it, but cultivate it.* " 'Hem," she murmured. "About the young fellow I mentioned, Lieutenant. Private Gant. As I said, I left him in a cave twenty miles to the west of here. I walked a good deal farther, of course, but that's about as the crow flies. I imagine that—"

"One moment," von Leibnitz said curtly, lifting his head. His pink nose twitched rabbit-like. He swung his head toward the pup-halves.

"*Sergeant!*"

"Yessir!"

"Take the name of whoever is smoking."

"Yessir."

McNair shook his head. "Isn't that a bit stiff, Karl? We're in bivouac, after all—"

"I gave a no-smoking order this morning, John. I have not countermanded it. You will go on, please, Miss Lee."

"I imagine," Cresta said a trifle doggedly, "that you can spare a couple of men to go after Private Gant. And I can guide . . ."

She let her voice trail because von Leibnitz was already shaking his head. "Oh no, no. It is out of the question. I am sorry."

Cresta Lee regarded him for a moment, her eyes turning softly smoky. "Don't think I quite caught you, Lieutenant. Would you mind—?"

"No, Madam!"

"Well," Cresta said ominously.

"It is not personal, you understand. It is my job." Von Leibnitz smiled synthetically. "I have very strict orders. I must pursue them. It is more important than one wounded soldier."

Cresta was getting angrier by the moment: she controlled her voice. "What orders are so important that you can't spare two lousy—two troopers out of fifty or so for a couple of days? Good Lord, Lieutenant! Honus Gant risked his life for me— for everyone in this territory! He's uncovered a gunrunner who could put the whole Northern Cheyenne nation back on the warpath."

"Miss, I note what you say. I will even commend this Trooper Gant in my report. But now, he must stay where he is. Later—"

"How much later?"

"I do not know." Von Leibnitz shrugged his pale comma-like brows. "It is the assignment. Maybe two days. Three. Maybe a week, maybe two—"

"Two!"

"Cresta," McNair said with a hint of worried urgency.

She came to her feet, bracing both fists on her hips. "Do I understand, Lieutenant, that the man who's probably saved this territory from a bloodbath will be left to die in a cave alone, for a fistful of stinking orders?"

"My dear Miss Lee—" Von Leibnitz' face turned a startled turgid hue. "Please! Do not mistake me. I want to help this man. I shall. But the assignment first. Meantime Gant is better off where he is. Think. We will be on patrol for perhaps weeks. We expect to engage the enemy. Now. Gant is hurt. How do you bring him to us? On a horse drag? Then he must ride in one of these wagons. Think of the punishment for a wounded man. Is this what you want?"

"No!" Cresta snapped. "I want you to send me and one or two others with food and a few medical supplies. We could stay with him till he's fit to ride. *If* you can't spare a man, give the stuff to me. I'll take it alone."

"No, Madam!" Von Leibnitz' face had screwed up till he looked like an apple-cheeked infant with the colic. "I will not permit it. You cannot go off by yourself, a young woman in this wild country. You will stay with the detail."

Cresta nodded very slowly, eying him as if she had just kicked over a rock and discovered him underneath. She was past all caution now. "Well. That is *damned big* of you, boy."

"I beg your pardon!"

"You should, you cheesefaced clown! Who the hell do you think you're talking to—some giggly milk-and-molasses society frump? I've been on my own out there for three days—pulling a wounded man through on my own for a week before that. For hell's sake! If I—"

"Cresta!" McNair said with a chill grimness.

He turned to von Leibnitz, who was staring at her with his jaw sagging over his collar. "Karl, will you leave us, please? I'd better speak with my fiancée alone."

Chapter Fourteen

After von Leibnitz' striker had gathered buffalo chips and
gotten a fire going, he poured a cascade of Santos coffee into
a pot and filled it with canteen water. He broke out an issue
chunk of fatty bacon and sawed it into irregular slabs that he
laid in a skillet, then set some stone-hard wafers of Army hardtack on a rock and pulverized them to crumbs with the butt
of his Colt—the only way that noble biscuit could be reduced
to an eatable consistency.

Cresta sullenly watched him stir the pebbly splintered crumbs
into the spitting grease—and listened to McNair's low, persuasive voice.

"Karl's not a bad chap, if you give him a chance—and,"
McNair smiled wryly, "get him away from von Steuben, the
Little Corporal and Bismarck. His idols."

"I don't get it. How did that parade uniform with a head
on its shoulders wind up out *here?*"

"Well, Karl's from an old Prussian family that expects great
things of him. That's Europe—old best-family tradition to seek
one's fortune in a foreign army. Romance of the West. Red
Indians. An uncle of his is the Austrian ambassador here, so
a West Point commission was wangled. But Karl's still un-
tried—hasn't served in a campaign, even a skirmish. His older

brother, Franz, was a hero of the Franco-Prussian War. Commanded a battery of artillery that broke the French charge at Weissenburg. What a thing for Karl to carry on his shoulders. If he doesn't make good, the old baron, his dad, will disown him. The result—he's unsure of himself, trying to cover it with lots of bark and ramrod, and doing his best under a great strain."

Cresta gave him a short glance. "Can I take it you like him?"

"I understand him, at least. You know how my family is. And I'm a kind of throwback myself—a gentleman soldier. I chose, even if I sometimes wonder why, to distinguish myself in the professional military—instead of in law, medicine, business, like the rest of my family. Officers in our army are generally of modestly well-to-do families—their career is a job, a matter of ambition and advancement. But Karl and I were born to wealth: with us, it's a heap more. Try to be a little tolerant with him, can't you?"

"Look," Cresta said flatly. "I'm not sharpening an ax for anybody. But Honus Gant needs help—and he's sure as hell earned it! I don't give a damn how important this mission is— that squarehead friend of yours could spare one or two out of fifty men to go with me!"

"He could," McNair agreed. "But you've made him mad now. If you'd kept quiet and let me do the arguing, I think he'd have been brought around. Now—" He shrugged. "I can only do my best to mend matters. Secure his co-operation. But I'm not sanguine. Not after my fiancée has sworn at him and called him a cheeseface."

Cresta grimaced. "Can't you give the order?"

McNair tapped one of his empty shoulder straps. "Not one that overrides his. He wears the bars. And this is his patrol. I am merely present as the voice of experience—Colonel Tabler's idea. Karl's sudden first lieutenancy is, after all, quite unearned. More grease from on high."

He paused, eying her soberly. "Just how bad off is this trooper of yours? Evidently he's well enough for you to leave him. You say he has some food—plenty of water. Granted, his situation's far from cozy—but in somewhat better than a pinch, he should survive for a couple of weeks."

"I suppose so," Cresta said a little sullenly. "It's just a damned dirty trick, that's all. What *is* this great mission of yours, anyhow?"

For answer, he took her by the arm and led her around to the back of the second wagon. He untied the canvas flaps and held them open.

Cresta peered inside. She saw three stubby, rather ungainly-looking guns mounted on wooden blocks. They appeared to be made of bronze, and were too small for cannon.

"What d'you call those?"

"Cohorn mortars. Will take up to an eight-ounce powder charge and will throw a seventeen-pound shell up to twelve hundred yards."

"For God's sake! What for?"

McNair shrugged. "Myself, I think a pair of Hotchkiss mountain guns on carriages would be the ticket, if you're going to lug artillery around on the plains. But the War Department wants these things tested more for plains fighting. Also we're the bait for the trap, so to speak—and the Cohorns are easily concealed in a single wagon. . . ."

"*What* trap?"

"For Spotted Wolf, believe it or not. Some genius had the idea that, since we're having hell's own time trying to run the Wolf into a corner, we've got to make him come to us. Since he's too cagey to attack a large force, our little detail was dispatched into the heart of his stamping grounds with this monstrosity of a wagon. Idea being that when he hits us, we lob a few explosive bonbons into his midst. *Voilà!*"

"Oh, for God's sake." Cresta Lee planted her fists on her hips. "That's crazy! In the first place, he's sure to smell a trap. In the second—he won't mass his men at a standstill for you to blow to pieces. Besides which, when he sees he's outgunned, he'll simply turn tail and run."

"I know it," McNair said wearily. "But some of our brassbound leaders back East haven't stirred off their *Cooke's Cavalry Tactics* in years."

"Well, I didn't *figure* an idea that imbecilic would come from General Crook's headquarters. Even the Cheyenne respect Old Three Stars."

"No, not Crook. Orders didn't come through Laramie. These were relayed directly from Omaha. No real harm in it, I suppose. We'll just bat around the plains for a few weeks, then go home."

"Huh. What does Lieutanent Schnickelfritz think—if anything—of all this?"

MCNair suppressed a smile as he secured the wagon flaps again. "Afraid Karl has visions of heroic stand-up battles against Rousseau's idealized savage. Which is, you understand, a befeathered European wearing a fringed breechclout and doing quaint pastoral things on a Gainesborughesque landscape. Karl's not stupid—not in the way the bald facts suggest. Just inexperienced in the way of any shavetail—and had the prior disadvantage of being reared in frozen forms of thought and tradition that no American born can appreciate. Being unsure of himself anyway, he naturally can't be disabused of his notions—things like breaking squares of infantry with cavalry charges; sort of thing that artillery—by which he paradoxically swears—made obsolete generations ago. . . . Well—shall we eat?"

They walked back to the fire. Sunset had slashed a scarlet blade across the pale flank of horizon. Twilight clung like a solemn burr to the plains. The troopers' fires were ruddy oases in the growing dimness.

Von Leibnitz' striker said: "S'all ready, Lootenant. Go ahead 'n' eat, you and y'r lady."

He had already loaded a plate, which he carried over to von Leibnitz, who sat on his heels some little distance off, aloof, refusing to look their way. McNair filled his own tin plate and coffee cup for Cresta; he shoveled the rest of the bacon and hardtack into a spare pan and ate from that, sitting cross-legged on the ground beside her.

Cresta took a sip of the Santos and shuddered. "I'd forgotten how a real cup of coffee tastes. Maybe I was lucky."

McNair chuckled. "Barracks rumor has it you make Santos by carefully charring horse apples, grinding them to splinters, and adding sulphate of quinine for flavor. It's not really as bad as all that—"

"But the way it's made, nobody can tell the difference."

"Right." McNair gingerly cracked a hunk of hardtack with his teeth. "Afraid Karl's in a real pet."

"Poor Johnny." She laid a hand on his arm. "I'm still embarrassing you, aren't I? Seems every time I get up another batch of good intentions about improving the Lee manner. all comes to nought. How do you wear me so well, anyhow?"

McNair smiled ruefully. "You do pinch a little in the tight places. And I did falter once . . . if you'll remember."

She wasn't likely to forget.

McNair had been fresh out of West Point when they had met. The meeting had culminated a long and nicely calculated campaign on Cresta's part. Later (for this was part of her code) she had frankly told him of her slum background, her orphanage upbringing, the years of painstaking study to improve her mind—and hard work to improve her station in life.

When she'd finally become the first assistant to one of Boston's leading seamstresses, it had put her in a position to maneuver a meeting with the young subaltern, who was then idling at home and waiting for his first assignment.

All had gone smoothly till the time had come for her to meet his family. Even the small subterfuges attempted by Johnny to blunt the impact of her non-society status hadn't dimmed the immediate hostility of his mother and three sisters. And Old Man McNair—the bawdy old fool—had made clandestine passes at her at every opportunity.

Things hadn't improved with time. The last straw had come when Mrs. McNair and her bitchy brood had invited Cresta to a gathering of their regular cackle club confreres and had spent the afternoon flaying her down to raw nerves with every dissecting blade of verbal malice they could command. And that

123

was considerable. Cresta, though, had served up a climax of her very own. It came when she had stood up and delivered herself of one calm, deliberate, devastating, well-chosen, two-word comment, then walked out in the dead silence.

She hadn't heard from Johnny for two months. The incident, she guessed, had proven far more than even he could swallow. She'd been nearly right.

When word did come, it was in the form of a long telegram from Jefferson Barracks near St. Louis. He had gotten assigned at last; he was on his way to Fort Reunion. Could she forgive him—and would she join him at once?

Cresta had pride, but she was also eminently sensible. She did not love Johnny McNair, but she began to respect him in that moment. He was eating humble pie for them both—and standing up to his strong-minded and domineering family (read Mother McNair) at the same time.

Of course she'd wired back an affirmative.

Johnny had sent his decision to *pater familias* too. Old Man McNair had begged her to come to his office, where he had tried to buy out her stock of marital ideas and had offered a bonus for a nice little arrangement on the side. She had laughed in his face and walked out. Within an hour she was on a train heading west. . . .

"It's been hell." McNair's head was bowed, his hands clenched around the edge of the pan. "I haven't stopped blaming myself these two years. If I'd had the courage to stand up to Mother and my sisters after the blowup—no, from the very first day I brought you to meet them—and then taken you west with me, what happened to you wouldn't have happened. Instead . . . my assignment to the Barracks arriving so damned opportunely, I seized on it as an excuse to run. From Mother. From you. From facing what had to be faced. I left Boston the night my orders came. Telling myself again and again that you deserved nothing from me. Not after humiliating the women of my family before their friends."

He sighed, shaking his head. "And don't think I couldn't guess what a damned setup they tried on you."

Cresta put her plate and cup aside and laid both hands on his shoulders. "Johnny, listen."

"All this time, not knowing. Imagining all the worst—oh, Cresta—"

She studied his face: the young, faintly lined, deep-weathered maturity of it. These two years on the plains had changed him. These, and whatever self-immolations he'd served on himself. She felt a wave of unexpected warmth toward him.

"Look here, Johnny. You *did* come through for me, didn't you? That's what matters. Nobody forced me to buy any tickets for the West. As for the Cheyenne, they were just my bad luck. The kind you can't rule out of the best-laid plan. Believe me—I know. Told you, didn't I, the way I schemed and worked just to meet you? I never denied my reasons. All right—blame? Then blame me."

"But . . ."

"Know something else, boy? You were strait-jacketed all your life by dear mater. You met me at about the age when young men who wear strait jackets shed 'em. And who was I? Somebody who could tell 'em all to go to hell. Fascinating, yes?"

"Come on," he protested. "That's not the only reason I asked you to marry me."

"No," she agreed dryly. "I generally do affect men other ways."

"You're not being fair! It has nothing to do with how I feel here and now."

She smiled faintly. "No? Just be sure you don't want me because you feel obligated now, Johnny."

McNair laid the pan aside and stood up. He held out both hands. She eyed him a dry, curious moment, then let him pull her to her feet. "If you're rested, let's walk a little. Maybe I can prove it to you. . . ."

They strolled away from the camp, walking slowly arm in arm. The dying day made a last flare of sickly ocher light across the hills. The land was cooling rapidly in the slow dusk, and she was glad of the greatcoat's warmth now. The voices of men and crickets made an oddly pleasing blend in the afterglow.

McNair cleared his throat quietly. "Cresta, I had no illusions about why you wanted to marry me. You were painfully frank—money. But it had to be more than that. I know that my governor offered you money."

"Your governor has a one-track mind," she said evenly. With a silent footnote: *in more ways than one.* "I don't give a damn about money that won't open doors. That's what's been denied me, Johnny, since I was born. It has to be a token. Not a bribe."

"I understand. He wouldn't, though." McNair paused, a little awkwardly. "At the same time, I felt that you did like me well enough—in the usual sense of that word."

"I did. I do, Johnny. Only—"

"Let me finish. Enough for love to come in time. Other people have started with as little, or less, and made good lives together. That is what I want with you, Cresta. A lifetime of loving. Maybe I'm a fool, but I thought it might come to be. I still do."

She walked in silence, her head down. How many women were lucky enough to be loved by a man of his character and kindliness? On her side of the tracks, men had seemed to become bastards in the normal course of things. Exactly as if they had never expected to be better, and women had expected no better of them. If Old Man McNair had been any example, prospects weren't a lot brighter among the silk underwear set.

"Cresta?"

"I can't say, Johnny. I just can't. It was all knocked out of me a long time ago. I *wish* I could. If you'll believe that. I don't understand you at all, my friend."

"What don't you?"

"What you see in me. Knowing just what a cold, greedy, ambitious—"

He laughed. "You cynical ones are all alike. You throw your own negative qualities into the worst light possible—and simply ignore your good ones."

"Oh, for God's sake. Hoh!"

"No, look," he said good-naturedly. "—courage, honesty,

forthrightness—so much that it's painful sometimes—and that fine inner toughness. A veritable gaggle of wholesome virtues."

Cresta tried to repress a rare reaction from her—a giggle—with the result that it erupted out of her almost explosively.

"And a sense of humor. Guess even the Cheyennes appreciated that."

She swallowed; she felt a small cold bristling. "Meaning what?"

"Why, nothing. They spared your life, that's all, Maheo bless them. And they don't appear to have treated you badly. Lordy, girl. Let a man offer up proper thanks to whatever deities . . ."

"I was a slave," she said stiffly, "to the family of the warrior who captured me. They treated me pretty well under the circumstances."

"Glad to hear that."

McNair sounded faintly mystified. By her defensiveness, she knew. A wash of guilty dismay swept her. Oh Lord. Why had she lied? She'd never dissembled to him before. O courage! O honesty! Where in hell were *hers* all at once?

It was the right thing, she had to insist in her bitter confusion. What good would it do for him to learn about Spotted Wolf? He loved her. It would only hurt them both. How long had she waited already? Why take a chance of throwing it all away. *Damn the code! You're sensible too. Be sensible.*

Only Honus Gant knew the truth—she'd been a fool to tell him so casually—but one cautioning word would ensure his silence. No need to worry about Honus.

Except in a quite different way.

"Johnny. Will you do as you said? Try to get von Leibnitz to send help to Honus Gant right away?"

"Cresta, I said I would. What's all this concern about Gant?"

She halted, pulling her arm out of the circle of his. "What's that supposed to mean?"

"Nothing, dear. I didn't—"

"I'm not to be trusted, is that it? I've been most of two weeks on the plains with Honus Gant, and most of the time we were alone. That what you're driving at? Well . . . ask

127

yourself all the questions, McNair. Let me know what you find out."

She turned and walked back toward the wagon.

"Cresta, please!"

She stopped, pressed a hand to her temple. Suddenly she hated herself. *Oh for—! What's the matter with you? First you get to lying, and now . . .*

She heard McNair's steps, felt his hands on her elbows, turning her to face him. "Darling, I'm sorry. I'm just another jealous male, I suppose. Don't blame a man for being normal. I promise I'll talk to Karl. Cresta?"

His hands lifted to her waist and pulled her close. She closed her eyes and tipped back her head, standing quietly in his arms as he kissed her eyelids, her lips, her throat. She felt the stirring of her natural hungers. His arms were a comfort too—and she was so damned tired of fighting life. There had to be more to it than that. Maybe she could learn to love him.

She slid her arms up around his neck, surrendering to the certainty of here and now—the fierce sweetness of lovers' kisses. The uncertainties diffused and lost their edges. For the time. . . .

Chapter Fifteen

Honus Gant was dreaming. A familiar dream of his, involving a little farm in Ohio. A liquid pattern of sunlight falling across a lush pasture that fat milch cows kept well cropped. The cows were lowing homeward ahead of him now, a spotted dog worrying their heels. A brass bell tinkled; wind whispered through oak leaves and carried the laughing voices of children from somewhere.

Ahead of him was a big red barn and whitewashed sheds. And beyond: a white farmhouse, rambler roses, a woman standing on the porch. She waved to him. She was slender and young—but her face stayed a nameless blur. (It was always enough to know that her yet hidden smile was for him, that her eyes would have the fine crinkles of much laughter at the corners: let a sometime reality fill in the rest.)

For once, though, that one thing about the picture bothered him. The girl's hidden face. He wanted to see it. If he could only get close! He fought with all his will to hold onto the dream a few more seconds. . . .

Even as he made the effort, it was dissolving and fading. With a wrenching sigh he gave it up and let go, and came suddenly awake in the gray chill light.

Rain? Unbelievable.

He scrambled to the tunnel mouth and peered out at the raw dripping dawn. A slow grin creased his face. In the few days since Cresta Lee had left him, the plains had been like a muggy open furnace, baked and scorched under the midsummer sun.

His fiercely itching leg was nearly healed. Sore as the devil yet, but he could hobble along fairly well with the aid of a crotched staff. Before she'd left, Cresta Lee had hacked it from a patch of scrub cottonwood she'd found growing upstream a ways.

Every day Honus had practiced with the improvised crutch till he'd developed a strong surging stride that put his full weight on his good leg and the staff, using only the toes of his hurt limb for balance. No need to wait till a party was sent from Fort Reunion: he was sure that he could make it out by himself.

He'd intended to start out this morning, sun or more sun—but tackling the plains in this blistering heat had been no pleasant prospect. It would sap his uncertain strength. Waterholes would be dry and game scarce. But he couldn't have remained in the cave another day, restless as he was.

He shouldn't have sent Cresta Lee back alone—that was the thought continually nagging his conscience. Maybe she'd been right, after all. Cumber might not even return to Fort Reunion.

Common sense ruled that he was being foolish. She was more capable than he of taking care of herself out there—in some ways anyhow. All the same, if she did run into danger, even his doubtful protection would be better than none.

Also—it shocked him a little to realize—he missed her bright and spicy presence. Even her tart tongue and her charming use of profanity.

First he'd told himself that way out here a man would miss any human companion, even one as aggravating as Cresta Lee. Then he wasn't so sure. He kept seeing her face, the sure and beautiful movements of her. He remembered the quick, strident way she talked. And gave himself a real shock, finally, when he found himself carrying on an imaginary argument with her.

That was it, Honus thought. Either it was the heat or he was going crazy. Either way, he was getting out of here. Maybe he couldn't overtake her or be of much help if he did, but he was going.

He had a pencil stub and a notebook he used to jot down thoughts of random and purely private interest. He tore out a leaf, scribbled a few lines of explanation—against the possibility that he wouldn't make it out—dated the note and left it pinned with a rock. He ruefully inspected the scraps of jerky that remained. They'd probably carry him through, but he was tired of constant hunger pangs and the monotonous jerky itself. Packing grub and his blanket in a single roll, he slung it with his canteen and Winchester across his shoulder, then crutched his way down the hill. After filling the canteen at the spring, he was on his way.

He swung steadily along through the light rain, luxuriating in the wet coolness that pasted his blouse to his back. He felt strong and free, almost lightheaded. Odd how muggy weather and just sitting around jaded a man's spirits—and how quickly they picked up on the move through a cool rain.

Tramping in it awhile filed the edge off his mood. An hour later, the rain still steadily falling, he was shivering wretchedly. He almost considered turning back to the cave. But before noon the rain quit; the sun dried him out and warmed him.

The plains rolled endlessly to every horizon. He had never felt their awesome impact quite as strongly as he did now—alone and pitting his lonely strength against their vastness.

It was still their country—the Indians'. What was your civilization, after all, way out here? A handful of towns and posts slenderly arteried by wagon ruts and the "whispering wires." Hardly scratches on this pristine immensity.

The Indians belonged. Great fighters, they had never found their Genghis Khan. The leader who might have welded their warring tribes into a red juggernaut that would smash the white man's tenuous toeholds on the continent and drive him into starving enclaves in his towns, all lines of supply and communication shattered.

Only Tecumseh had entertained the idea to any breadth.

And it was far too late, now, for another Tecumseh. It was too late even for a Spotted Wolf. But if Spotted Wolf did succeed in lighting a fire under the Northern Cheyennes, the dust would be a long time a-settling. . . .

Honus tramped into the afternoon, halting often to rest. Though the steady rain didn't resume, the day was plagued by intermittent showers. He began to hit little scattered mottes of oak which, if he happened to be near one, provided shelter from the sudden rains.

Sometimes he tested his healing leg, letting it take the gingerly weight of a full stride or two. The muscles responded well, sore as they were. Again he marveled at Cresta's poultices.

He thought about her a good deal. He thought about other things too, but his thoughts kept swinging back like a magnetic needle to a lodestone. He kept scanning the horizon, knowing he would not see her, yet expecting to at any moment.

Annoyed, he pushed his will against the odd reflex. He went over everything that Cresta Lee was, then everything she wasn't, just to prove how ridiculous it was. Good God, no two people could be less alike!

Her kind of man? No need to guess twice. What she'd told him about Lieutenant John McNair: *twice your size . . . ten times as smart . . . good-looking.*

Honus began to feel, quite unbidden, a quiet hatred for Lieutenant John McNair, whom he had never met. Not, he told himself, for any reason outside of general principles. It was only that it smarted, having Cresta Lee throw it up to him just that way. Why shouldn't it? Any boy who'd been homely, awkward, miserably shy with girls, learned to resent the big, handsome, easy-mannered ones who took whatever they wanted so easily.

All the same—the further he pursued this line of thinking, the more uneasy it made him.

In fact, he had an instant of conscious relief as the clear sharp report of a rifle hit his ears. The sound wiped everything else straightway from his mind.

Honus paused, listening. He faced an undulating rim of hill

—the shot seemed to have come from beyond it. He awkwardly unslung the Winchester and held it in his right hand, using his left to maneuver the crutch as he scaled the hill.

He reached the top. A jungle of scrub oak rambled away below him, spreading out in irregular tatters and clusters. There was movement down there, a crackle of twigs.

Suddenly a deer burst clear of the fringing scrub and tore into the open. It streaked for the slope. Honus (no hunter, he)—in the combined reflex of an empty gut and seeing a hundred-plus pounds of fresh meat on the hoof—threw his rifle to his shoulder and fired.

He stood incredulous. Because it had been the hastiest and clumsiest of shots (he needing both hands to hold the rifle while simultaneously crutch-braced), he'd expected nothing. Yet the powdersmoke had shredded away and a dead buck was stretched at the base of the slope.

"I got him—I got him!"

The only trouble was, there seemed to be another hunter about. Friendly or hostile? That was the big question.

Honus went down the hill slowly, raking the line of oak woods with his eyes. He had nearly reached the deer when a man stepped almost noiselessly out of the trees.

A stocky Indian. He was wearing a mixture of white and Indian garb, including a ludicrous plug hat. His carbine was up and ready.

He faced Honus across the carcass of the dead buck. The whole look of him proclaimed hostility. Worse. It said that he had marked this buck for his own, and would the white man care to try conclusions?

"I don't think you'd have gotten him," Honus said reasonably, "but there's enough to go around, isn't there? Only trouble is, how do I explain it so you'll understand? Hmm. Any English? Eng-lish?"

The Indian's eyes were like small black stones.

Honus smiled disarmingly. "You—me—friends, eh? We share, okay?" He pointed to the Indian, to himself, to the buck. And moved the edge of his palm in a slicing motion, as with a knife.

It took some doing, but aided by a weird contrivance of gestures and a few English words that it turned out the Indian knew, they achieved communication. Honus got across that he only wanted a venison steak or two, a little·grub to take along, and some information.

He did what he could to help the Indian gut, bleed, skin and cut up the animal. They carried the quarters to the Indian's camp, where his woman whacked off hefty portions for broiling. Their little boy admired Honus' pocketknife so much that he gave it to him for good will's sake. He felt trepidation when the boy promptly cut his hand on the large blade, but neither parent seemed concerned.

After eating, Honus smoothed a patch of ground and scratched lines on it with a stick. A full belly and Honus' generosity with venison and knife had melted the Indian's stony reserve. He turned voluble and expressive. He talked, violently gestured, and added more lines to Honus' crude map.

At the end of an hour, Honus had a pretty clear picture of what the man knew. Cresta Lee had encountered this same family the day after she had left the cave—at a point about halfway between the Indians' present camp and Janroe River. The Indian had told her of a cavalry patrol they had met coming up from the southeast. Concerning this, she had seemed very interested, but he did not know what she had done then.

Knowing Cresta, Honus gambled that she'd change her route to overtake the wagon-burdened patrol. Even in the several days that had elapsed since she and the Indians had met, the patrol could not have traveled far.

Honus knew the direction in which they were heading; he could loosely compute their rate of travel. He could cut across-country to intersect their route at a point very close to where they'd be.

As a matter of fact, provided they'd held a roughly straight course, they shouldn't be more than a day's trek from here by now. No reason he couldn't find them too.

The Indian, though still friendly, was starting covetously to eye Honus' Winchester. Which seemed like an excellent cue on which to take his departure.

He didn't cover much ground the rest of that day. It kept showering off and on, the sun ducking behind thick clouds. Getting periodically drenched was not only no fun, the paucity of landmarks made the lack of sun for guidance a real problem.

The weather cleared entirely by sunset, which gushed across the sky like a gouting wound. He kept its scarlet welt at his back as he tramped on. Darkness brought a skyful of familiar constellations and the fixed assurance of the North Star to keep at his left shoulder.

The air was cool, but not unpleasantly so, and incredibly fresh. Tramping endlessly on by starlight, he felt almost tireless, strangely buoyant with the night's beauty, his leg giving him almost no trouble.

Not till after midnight was he aware of the warning cramps in his muscles that told him to stop—rest.

It came to him as he was sitting on a hill's star-silvered crown and resting, still filled with that vast sense of buoyancy and attributing it to nature and the night.

Why in hell was he trying to overtake the patrol anyway? If Cresta Lee had already found them, they could send a messenger to Fort Reunion. That was taken care of, and he might as well strike on for the fort.

Only—suppose something had happened to Cresta? For example? Well, how should he know? An accident—anything. And suppose it had, what could he do?

He didn't get any further with the sterile self-debate because the fact ballooned through his brain at that instant. *Good Lord. By Gadfrey, I'm in love with that girl.*

He thought it all over very carefully. Nothing but trouble, he decided, could come of loving a girl like Cresta Lee. Oddly the thought didn't depress him. All he knew was that he was going to find her soon and that he felt like tackling lions.

He stretched out, arms folded under his head, and watched the stars. He slept after a while. And had the dream again. But the girl's face was no longer a blur. Misplaced as it might be, she wore the face of Cresta Lee. And it seemed painfully right that she should.

Chapter Sixteen

Lieutenant Karl von Leibnitz was very much out of countenance with Miss Cresta Lee—as usual. Riding alongside the mortar wagon where she sat perched on the driver's high seat, he mopped his sweating face with a bandanna and glared at her.

"Henceforth, Miss, I shall ask you to confine yourself to the vicinity of this wagon when we make evening camp and not go showing yourself about the camp in that—that disreputable wardrobe."

Cresta glanced down at her disreputable wardrobe. It consisted of Johnny's spare military blouse, baggily oversized except across her bosom, and a pair of his yellow-striped trousers which she had stagged off a few inches above her ankles. She'd retained her battered straw hat, and knew she made quite a picture.

"I don't know what to do about it, Lieutenant. Unless you happen to have a complete lady's outfit in your saddlebags. Except I doubt that you'd have much knowledge, intimate or otherwise, of—"

"Madam!"

"All right, all right, keep your saber scar on. I don't like you either. If you have any other point to make around all that meal in your mouth, for God's sake get it out."

"You compel me." Von Leibnitz' china-blue eyes were icy. "You have a blatant immodesty of appearance, speech and manner which I find offensive in a young woman. In an officer's fiancée, I find it revolting. You display none of the reticence nor decorum I should expect—"

"Oh for God's sake!"

McNair was riding the length of the column from its rear; he moved up on the trot beside the wagon.

"Anything wrong, Karl?"

"What could be wrong?" von Leibnitz piped in his flat harried accent. He wheeled his mount back toward the head of the column.

McNair glanced at the stolid teamster who sat beside Cresta, cudding a wad of plug cut and totally indifferent to all the byplay.

"Kelly, I'll take your place awhile. Take my horse and pull back a ways. Think we can change without halting the detail?"

"Aye, sir."

Kelly gave McNair a hand as he stepped gingerly from his stirrup across the wheel. After passing the lieutenant his reins, Kelly seized McNair's reins and vaulted lightly into his saddle. Holding the animal in, he fell back some paces behind the wagon.

It took McNair an awkward minute or so to get the feel of the team. Then he glanced at her, his eyes crinkling at the corners.

"I was about to say you look like an urchin. But there are a few salient differences. Thank goodness."

"I know. It has that beet-faced refugee from Heidelberg all bothered."

McNair smiled, though a little worriedly. "I wish you'd try not to chafe Karl. I know he tempts one to round on him now and then, but . . ."

Cresta brooded through half-lidded eyes at the dusty rumps of the wheel mules. Uninspired, she raised her gaze to the square blue shoulders of von Leibnitz out ahead of the double-columned detail. *Either way,* she mused, *you're looking at a mule's ass. What a depressing thought.*

She had thought the uncertainties of the other night would resolve themselves after a few days of McNair's company.

They hadn't. If anything, they had intensified. The worst of it was, she couldn't understand what was wrong with her. For the first time in her life, Cresta Marybelle Lee felt unsure of herself. And it frightened her.

The two wagons and the pack train were placed roughly toward the detail's center. The second wagon, so she had learned, contained shells and accessories for loading the mortars: these extras equaled the total weight of the weapons themselves.

It was late in the day. Cresta's backside ached from jouncing for ten hours on a hard seat. She felt in no mood for even a mild bawling out. Sore as her neck was, she twisted her head to stare across the heat-dancing plains. They humped away to the horizon, yellow-quilted with timothy and grama hay that, in some places, stood belly-high to a tall horse.

By now the detail was deep inside the broad range that Spotted Wolf's movements usually covered. Again she thought dourly of just what a damned stupid waste of time this expedition was.

Especially with Honus Gant alone in that cave, needing help.

Mechanically her gaze pinpointed the saffron rim of hills just below the dipping sun. Beyond them was the rocky range and the cave and Honus. . . .

Damn damn damn! She balled a small fist on her knee. Why couldn't she shake herself free of this nagging (and probably baseless) worry for him? She had done all she could, for God's sake! What else could she do?

The trouble was, with nothing better than getting beaten sore on a wagon seat to occupy her, she found her mind enlarging on all kinds of uneasy possibilities. Suppose (for example) that that stubborn damned fool decided he was well enough to tackle the long empty miles to Fort Reunion by himself? Ye gods! He was no plainsman. If he didn't get

himself good and lost the first day, it would be a crying miracle.
And with his unique powers of marksmanship, it was just a
question of how long it would take him to starve to death. . . .

"Uh, Johnny? Listen. You think you could have another try
at Schnickelfritz? About Gant—"

"Oh Lord," McNair said wearily. "Cresta, what do you expect
of me? You know I've approached Karl three times already."

"I know, Johnny. But—"

"It's no dice, I tell you. Gant stays where he is till the
mission's concluded. I've not only managed to annihilate whatever friendship Karl and I had, he's cited me in his report—
for attempting to obstruct his orders. . . ."

"Oh, for—! You're not serious!"

"You should know Karl by now." McNair glumly shook the
reins and clucked at the mules. "Look, dear. I've tried—repeatedly. I've more than kept my promise. Now I want yours."

Cresta said guardedly: "What's that?"

"I want your word not to bring up Honus Gant again in
any way . . . till this mission's been brought to some sort of
conclusion. And that includes any pretty scheme of taking
things into your own hands. Don't look innocent! And don't
deny it hasn't crossed your mind . . . going to Gant on your
own."

"John, old boy. You *are* jealous. . . ."

"No, dammit! All right—maybe I am. Not because I think
there was anything between you and Gant. But because I know
only too well what goes on in that lovable stubborn head of
yours. That once you've taken an idea in it and someone says
no, you're like as not to damn 'em and go ahead just . . .
just because."

"Hmmm." Cresta rubbed her nose with a grubby palm.
"Think so?"

"Look, dear." He made his voice low and persuasive. "You
and Gant went through a good deal together. I understand
that, and I respect your loyalty to a comrade. But Gant is a
soldier. He understands that he's paid to take whatever risks
his duty demands. I only hope that I could perform over and

above the call as well as you tell me Gant has. Now . . . what about you?"

"What d'you mean?"

"You're going to be my wife. You have a duty to me—you have to start thinking in those terms. If you follow your whims—make me sick with worry . . . Cresta, is it asking too much that you put me and our interests first in your thoughts?"

"No." She looked down at her hands. "It's not too much, Johnny."

"Then—how about your word?"

"All right." Her hands curled achingly together in her lap. "I promise."

The patrol made camp in the chaparral under a looming black range of hills. Cresta lay sleepless in her blankets under the wagon, twisting on a fakir's spike-bed of the soul.

The uncertainties again. Swarming in her brain worse than ever. Why had she given Johnny that damned promise? And what did that have to do with it anyway?

She pressed her hand to her hot forehead, trying to think. Where had the feeling begun, anyhow? Hadn't it been about the time she had told Johnny the lie—half-truth—about her captivity? *Half-truth, hell.* She'd as good as lied.

'Fess up. That's what's wrong. You haven't the belly for lying. And then resignedly: *You might as well get it all out now. You're just not made so you can keep it in.*

About two hundred feet from the wagon, a lone sentry paced his watch, rifle shouldered, back and forth through a sultry dance of firelight. Other sentinels were posted at opposite sides of the camp, Cresta knew. McNair was making the rounds of their posts, and now she saw him come up to the fire, halt, speak briefly to the sentry, then head this way.

He walked softly past the wagon toward his own blankets. Cresta raised herself on an elbow, saying quietly, "Johnny."

He halted and came back, dropping down on one knee beside her. "Thought you'd be asleep."

"Johnny . . ." She looked at the hand she held lightly

clenched around the blanket folds. "Have you thought of when we get back? To the fort, I mean. Or for that matter, to any future posts where you're assigned. . . ."

"I think I know," he said gently.

"Do you? John-boy, no matter where you're transferred, the story will go along too. Your wife was with the Cheyennes. Think about it. Then think about your career."

"Cresta. People talk and burros bray. It's all one. Why should it matter, a lot of nasty speculation?"

"Suppose, John . . . suppose all that speculation were right on the head?"

McNair peered at her sharply. He started to smile. The smile faded as he saw what she was telling him. His hand was resting on his knee, and she saw it tighten till even in the ruddy dimness the knuckles showed white.

"I was Spotted Wolf's wife. His youngest squaw, if you prefer. For nearly a year. I held out against it for a year before that. Then it would've been my neck. So I underwent puberty rites, became a Cheyenne woman . . . and married Spotted Wolf."

McNair lowered his head till the flesh of his neck grooved whitely against his collar. "I don't care."

"Don't you, Johnny?"

He looked at her directly. She saw that his eyes were steady again. "What made you decide to tell me?"

"Oh, I don't . . . yes, I do. One thing—I'd never lied to you. And I can't spend a lifetime pretending to be what I'm not—as I've pretty well proved with Schnickelfritz."

"Then don't!" His voice shook with intensity. "Be what you are, Cresta. If I ever say anything again . . ."

She reached up and touched his cheek. "Johnny," she murmured. "Don't you understand, Gentleman John? I'm damaged goods. Not the greedy but virtuous little hardnose you met in Boston. That's what I'm saying."

"But you couldn't help it, Cresta!"

"It doesn't change the fact."

."The fact doesn't matter."

"Oh, it does. You're a remarkable fellow, John . . . even I didn't realize how remarkable. But it does matter. Or will. And you know why."

"All right." He grasped her hand tightly. "It does. It matters that people will talk, true or not. And now I know the truth, and that matters too. I am worried about what people will think and say. I'm worried for your sake, but on my account too. And I love you, Cresta, and I need you. And that makes it all worth it. I know this means very little to you—which also matters, and none of it changes a damn thing. I still love you. I always will."

She felt her eyes start to blur. His words affected her more than she'd have believed possible. She didn't love McNair, but that he loved her meant something . . . where it hadn't before. It was important, she thought suddenly, to be cared for. Was that, really, all that did matter? If only it were!

She pressed his hand where it covered hers. "Johnny dear, I'm honored. Deeply honored. But don't you see? Even if I could learn to care for you—that way—it wouldn't work. There *is* your career. And there *is* your family. You can't just—"

"I can and I will," McNair said forcefully. He bent and kissed her forehead. "Go to sleep, darling. We'll talk again . . . but it's going to work out. You'll see."

He rose and walked to his bedroll, sat down and tugged off his boots, and rolled into his blanket.

Cresta lay on her side, pillowing her head on her folded arm; she stared at McNair's blanket-covered back. Damn! Confession hadn't relieved her by an iota. Good God! Trying to talk him out of an arrangement she'd gone through several hells to promote. She'd never deceived herself that this was a love match— why should it matter now?

She tossed for another hour, her head splitting with the pressure of doubts that wouldn't be put down.

Finally decision came.

A relevant decision? She didn't know. All she knew was that once she'd made it, she felt an instant flood of relief. To do *something!* Something she wanted to, whether it was right or wrong, whether it made sense or didn't.

She raised herself carefully to a sitting position. She could still see the sentry's dark form pacing, but his small fire had died low, its cherry glow no longer reaching out to the wagons.

Shortly she fumbled for her .45—Honus'—and her hat. Then she pushed her blankets aside and rolled out between the wheels on the side away from the sentry. Easing to her feet, she stole catlike around to the rear of the wagon and undid the pucker flaps.

Moving with infinite care, she climbed into the wagon box and rummaged noiselessly about, locating all that she would need by feel. No problem: the two officers had stashed their own effects in this wagon, and in preparing Johnny's meals and keeping his possibles neatly arranged, she'd been in and out a score of times.

Outside of a good supply of grub, she'd need little. A blanket, a canteen of water, quinine barks (in case needed) and a cartridge box of .45 shells. She set it all in the blanket and made a bundle by knotting the four corners together.

She left the wagon like a small shadow, slipping to the ground and crossing swiftly to the edge of the camp. She halted for a brief backward glance at the sleeping forms of McNair and von Leibnitz, whose continual snoring had helped to cover any chance noise she'd made.

I'm sorry, Johnny. It was a bad promise. I've got to, that's all.

She knew exactly where the sentries were posted. Their stations had been chosen with an eye to picking up anybody attempting to enter the camp, not one who meant to leave it.

The picket line wasn't covered. Cresta slipped along it. The horses were unperturbed, as she'd guessed, by her familiar scent.

She ducked under the picket rope and out into the chaparral, moving quickly and quietly in her tough rawhide moccasins. The stars picked out her way, laying a whitesilver sheen on

144

the prairie grass except where the inky clots of brush made irregular patches.

It was unlikely that she'd be missed till early morning. Even if she were, they couldn't follow her by darkness, and by dawn she'd be miles away.

Johnny? Whatever he might say or wish, Lieutenant Schnickelfritz would permit no side expeditions to hunt for a foolish girl. In fact, Schnickelfritz would have reason for self-congratulation. Had he not expressly forbidden her to leave the detail? *Ja!* Foolish, foolish girl!

She felt one more stab of regret. Poor Johnny. And not an excuse in the world for treating him so.

Except one. Honus Gant needed help. Or so she kept assuming, she thought irritably—why be so sure? No matter why. She was going straight back to him, a good store of food and medicine in her bundle. Too bad she couldn't have taken a horse, but that would have meant rousing the camp.

. Anyway it was good to be swinging out under the stars at her familiar trot—she was surprised at how good it felt. Was it that, or the starlight, or—what a thought—just getting away from Schnickelfritz? She didn't know the reason, but she felt absurdly lighthearted.

The brush thickened ahead, but just beyond was open prairie. Cresta began thrusting her way past the midnight masses of thicket. Abruptly she heard—or felt—movement off to her right.

She stopped, listening. No sound. But there'd been *something!* Her scalp prickled; her heart thudded in her chest.

Suddenly bushes rustled behind her.

Cresta began to wheel, opening her mouth to yell. A flat hard palm was slapped across her face; she was crushed powerfully against a man's chest. She squeaked off a half-yip before the hand clamped down over her mouth, throttling the sound. . . .

Chapter Seventeen

Long before noon, the sun was a broiling fury against their necks and right sides. The detail sweltered and suffered, bitched and swore its way across the summer plains.

Only Lieutenant John McNair showed no hint of discomfort. He sat his McClellan torture rack straight as a board, rocking to his mount's gait with the horseman's immemorial ease. The prickly sweat under his faded double-breasted shirt was an unending torment, but he never lifted a hand to rub or scratch; even when a horsefly settled on his chin and crawled up to his temple, he didn't twitch a muscle.

Dignity? Some of it was—quite aside from the numbness in his guts. He was a gentleman born and a cavalry officer trained, a combination that made for a fantastic degree of self-mastery. That was how it was. You were not supposed to feel what the common tackies did; if you couldn't help feeling it, you were not to show it by the bat of an eyelash. So that McNair, ordinarily an expressive and animated man, could be measured for the content of his agitation by the inverse hardening of his young face.

Just now, his features were like metal.

There'd been no glossing over the facts. Cresta Lee had not been spirited off against her will. Nor had she vanished into thin air. She had voluntarily appropriated provisions and cartridges and had sneaked out of camp. No camouflaging her reason either: she had willfully broken her given word not to go to Gant. . . .

While the troop was taking breakfast, McNair had made a hasty search of the camp area, calling Cresta's name and holding to a wispy tendril of hope that things weren't as they looked. But even a cursory look-around was enough to confirm that she was long gone. No time, though, to hunt track and fix her direction, for Leibnitz was already ordering the men to saddle.

Say what else you might about Karl, he was a gentleman. He'd avoided making any comment that would slip the needle deeper. But McNair knew what he was thinking—what some of the troopers were saying in *sotto voce* mutters. As McNair had told Cresta, he did care what people thought: the deep prod of his shame nearly equaled the hurt of betrayal. . . .

The plains simmered like the saffron roof of hell. On stretches where the dead grass had fallen to powder, dust bannered up in choking yellow clouds that even the suggestion of an air current was enough to raise. The men knotted bandannas over noses and mouth. Rest halts were made miserable by the horses' loud runny voidings, filling the air with a carrion-like stench.

As the day wore on, McNair's thoughts loosened up somewhat. Was he assuming too much . . . or too little? First he'd thought that she might be in love with Gant. But no, she'd have told him as much. That was Cresta's way. Sure, she might have lied in giving him a promise she'd had no intention of keeping—but more likely she'd given her word in all sincerity at the time. Which did not, of course, change the fact that she'd broken it. . . .

His mind was running in slow and vicious circles when the attack came.

The detail was crossing a monotonous stretch of country that was neither more nor less rolling or hilly or brush-covered than numerous other areas they'd traversed. Just an easy sweep of brush-pocked rises, and off to their right one big conical hill which had wheeled majestically in their perspective through the long day and was now quite close.

The troopers were relaxed, if not downright soporific. Too many uneventful days had gone before; today's dead cloying heat had them sleepy and irritable. There were no flankers out. The scouts had reported in at midmorning and, after describing the terrain ahead, hadn't gone out again.

One instant all was quiet. The next, rifles were popping on every side. Coppery shadows were darting out of the brush around the column, firing, running from thicket to thicket, firing again.

McNair drew his revolver and waved it above his head, at the same time turning his mount and bolting back down the demoralized line of troopers. He bawled a volley of orders above the roar of gunfire, the yells of men.

"Ride! Ride out of here, men! At the gallop—*ride out!*"

For a half minute or so, it was total chaos. Some men were scrambling off their horses to make a stand here; others were kicking their animals into flight.

Then McNair's words, shouted over and over, had their effect: that and the fact that there was no cover available here. Firing at whatever targets presented themselves, they climbed back in saddle and headed after their comrades.

McNair raced his mount back and forth, shouting the order over and over, adding another to it: "Get to the hill, men! We'll regroup there! Ride for the hill—"

It was the only course that made sense. That first unexpected salvo had broken their ranks to confusion. No way of telling the size of the enemy force or how many braves might be held in reserve—to hunt down and pick off the scattered troopers as they broke free of the trap.

With no cover available here, all they could do was ride blindly free of the murderous crossfire, each man for himself, then pull back together on an established vantage where a defense of sorts might be made. . . .

Mounted and yelling at the top of his voice, McNair became

a target for more than his share of lead. He was also amazingly lucky. A bullet whipped his sleeve; another gave his foot a numbing blow when it smashed the stirrup. Another creased his sorrel, and McNair had all he could do to haul the rearing, pawing animal down.

A brave chose that moment to dart at him from the side, his lance poised. He ran close, intending to count coup. McNair pointed his revolver and shot him in the chest from less than two yards away. The Cheyenne's painted face distorted; he arched over in a back-slamming fall under the bullet's impact.

Tight-reining his sorrel around, McNair looked for von Leibnitz in the fog of powdersmoke and the general confusion. He knew that his superior had been up front of the detail, well ahead of McNair, when the shooting had begun. No sign of him anywhere. . . .

The troopers who were able to ride were out of it now, all but a few. McNair started to ride after them, then remembered the wagons.

Once more he reined around, but pulled up almost at once. There'd be no getting the wagons out: the Indians had directed a fiercely deliberate fire at the two vehicles. Both teamsters were sprawled across their seats. The mules had gone down quickly, killed at once or kicking in a tangle of harness.

Hugging his mount's withers, McNair slammed in his spurs and veered away into the brush. Some panicked troopers had been cut down as they stampeded for the open. Using the scattered thickets as best he could, McNair frustrated any sharpshooters. Once he leaped his mount over a trooper's still form. A few yards on he saw another man stagger to his feet, blood pouring down his face from his gashed scalp. He looked dazed.

"Here, man!"

McNair slowed and pivoted his horse alongside, throwing out an arm. The trooper grasped it and swung up behind. Then they were riding clear of the ambush. . . .

Their casualties hadn't been as many or as serious as McNair had reckoned at first.

True, they had been lax and careless in thrusting their collective head into Spotted Wolf's noose. They'd all been worn ragged by monotony and heat, but that was no excuse. Not at least on the part of the two officers, who should have had the sense to keep out flankers and scouts, no matter how tranquil things had looked.

For Leibnitz—unseasoned and chockful of outlandish ideas about Indians and the way they fought—there might be some excuse. For himself, McNair thought, there was no excuse at all. Of course he'd warned Leibnitz to maintain all precautions, but he should have hammered the point home with a threat of Colonel Tabler's wrath.

It was pure luck that the Indians had not acted much less clumsily. Spotted Wolf's warriors, doubtless expecting another easy bloodletting, had gotten carried away. Rushing out to score coup at the very outset, they'd exposed themselves foolishly to the troopers' fire. Demoralized as they were, the soldiers had mowed down enough Cheyenne in that first charge to leave the battle evenly joined for the moment.

As McNair had guessed, Spotted Wolf had held a solid half or more of his force out of the action, stationing them beyond a line of knolls to the north. This second wave now charged, expecting an easy pick-off of scattered pony soldiers. But the troopers, heeding McNair's command, fell back toward the cone-shaped promontory to the east.

The hill was largely covered with a sparse and spiny chaparral which thinned out toward its top. It was studded with great chunks of shale, and the flat crown was literally rimmed by giant slabs, a natural breastwork.

The troopers piled hurriedly off their mounts. Following McNair's crisp order, they took up positions behind the rocks. The first line of warriors streamed up the rise, howling like demons.

"Aim for the horses this time," McNair said. "Make every shot count, boys. Fire at will!"

The bitter barrage cut down a half-dozen ponies, spilling their riders in the rocks. The rest wheeled with a beautiful precision and retreated. Four of the downed braves limped after them; two others lay unmoving where they had fallen.

McNair made a hasty count of his men, relieved to find that his early estimate of casualties could be downgraded. They had lost five in the ambush. Eleven had been wounded, only two seriously.

One of the two was Lieutenant Karl von Leibnitz.

Hit in the first volley, he'd been pulled practically from under a Cheyenne scalping knife by his striker, Private Robbins, who had gotten them out on his own horse, supporting the wounded officer.

Robbins, who had a fair degree of medical skill, was the company's fill-in surgeon. He had already tied off Leibnitz' wound with bandages taken from one of the two supply mules that the troopers had managed to pull out of the trap. Now he was tending the other injured men.

McNair moved along the line of dug-in men, crouching low, telling them to hold their present posts. When he came to von Leibnitz, lying on his back in the shadow of a slabby boulder, he halted and knelt down.

Von Leibnitz' blouse was open, his thick chest wrapped in bandages. His face was pasty and glistening.

"It is too late to say I am sorry, John. I should have listened."

"I should have made you listen. That was my job."

"No, John. No. How many?"

"We only lost five. But it's a bad situation, Karl. We're out all but two of the mules—and neither of 'em has a waterbag on him. We've only the water in our canteens, and almost no grub."

"*Ach.* That is bad. And the wagons with the mortars and the shells?"

"Had to abandon both." McNair paused, his sweat-tracked face squinting. "Must have wanted to immobilize them, the way they went after the harness mules."

"Did they know about the mortars, then?"

"Don't see how. I'd hazard that Spotted Wolf was curious

about those wagons. Probably guessed at a trap, from the size of our detail—that the wagons were part of it."

"So it is Spotted Wolf's band, this one."

"Several of our men say they saw him in the charge." McNair dropped a hand to von Leibnitz' shoulder. "Excuse me, Karl."

He moved on around the cordon of troopers, seeing that all sides of the hill were covered. He ordered a picket line strung between two slabs. The horses would be skittish from thirst before too long, when renewed gunfire might be enough to spook them.

The men had a hundred rounds apiece for their carbines, half in their belt-boxes and half in the saddlebags. None of the mules burdened with the reserve ammunition had gotten out.

McNair got his fieldglasses and trained them on the flats below. Apparently Spotted Wolf was converging his whole band on the hill, deploying his warriors around it in loose clots. Since the troopers' fire had broken the mounted charge, there was no sign that the Cheyennes would renew the attack at once.

McNair singled out Spotted Wolf. He had briefly met the war chief at a Laramie peace parley two years ago. Now, at Spotted Wolf's order, some braves were gathering brush and building a large fire.

For a moment McNair was puzzled. But only for a moment. The damned beggars intended to fire the brush on the hill. They held bunches of dead limbs in the flames, dispersed swiftly along the foot of the hill and thrust the ignited branches into masses of brush.

That was how Spotted Wolf had engineered the Battles massacre, McNair knew. A brush fire probably wouldn't work here, though. The wind would shoot the fire uphill, but not quickly. The brush was too thin, too green, and petered out altogether toward the rim.

On top of that, the wind changed after a few minutes and blew choking clouds of oily greenwood smoke back at the

Cheyennes. They hastily cleared off that side of the hill to let it burn out. An hour later it had fizzled down to a few trailers of smoke and a blackened cut on the hillside.

Fire wouldn't do the job. But all it meant was that the Cheyennes would have to lay siege till a few waterless days broke the enemy's resistance.

McNair went his rounds of the men again. A cheery word here—a stern one there. They responded well; they knew and liked McNair as "one goddam fine second looey" against the tenet of brassbound hatred for officers. He'd been with his own troop since his first assignment, and he knew they'd ride through hell for him. He was depending on that trust to keep morale high until the last possible hope had run out. And he used any halfway logical-sounding lies as catalysts toward that end.

Again he turned his glasses on the tableau below, training them on the ink-blue worm of water that straggled east-west across the flats and flushed in a turbulent current past the rocky north base of the hill.

Von Leibnitz husked, "What is it now, John?"

"They're bringing up their women and children," McNair muttered. "Converging around the stream. Baggage, lodgeskins, poles, packs, travois ponies. The works. I expect they'll simply wait us out—however long it takes."

"Is there not a chance that Spotted Wolf might withdraw?"

"I wouldn't bet a nickel on it. Matter of face. A handful of us holding off his band. He can't quit—not and hold his young men. Anyhow he won't have to wait long. Not if—"

McNair broke off, intent on the scene below.

"What, John?"

"Looks as if a passel of the bucks are drumming up a fight dance. Not a scalp dance—that'd come afterward. By God. I think they're boning up for another charge."

"But that is suicidal! We have the cover—all the advantage—"

"The young bloods. A Cheyenne warrior's his own man. Spotted Wolf won't be able to hold the young ones back if their blood's high. Likely he won't try, except for raising a token objection. Then when they get chopped to pieces, it'll be a solid endorsement for his wisdom. . . ."

The attack came just before sunset.

The troopers poured a constant shattering fire into the Cheyennes as they poured in thin ragged waves up the incline. They fired so rapidly that the barrels of the Springfields grew unbearably hot: cartridges swelled and jammed in the breeches. They had to hack at the empty casings with their knives in order to clear for reloading.

The young braves had worked themselves into a pellmell frenzy. For a short time the ferocity of their attack was such that the outcome swayed in the balance. They charged mounted, they charged afoot, scalps at their belts and breechclout flaps tied up for cartridge pockets. Some got so close before the slaughtering fire downed them that you could see the fuzzing of moiled dust on their oil-bright warpaint. Most of the time, the scene was half-obscured by the white blossoms of powdersmoke that frayed sullenly off on the slow air currents.

When they fell back for good, not a single of the Cheyenne dead or wounded were left behind. A kind of thunderous silence hung over the hot scape. It was gradually, almost cautiously broken by the numbed, exhausted mutters of the men.

McNair sank wearily back against a rock. It was like a red-hot plate on his rear; he swore and shifted away. Then sat cross-legged on the ground.

"How are you making it, Karl?"

Von Leibnitz opened his eyes, smiling wanly. "It is not too painful." A deprecating grimace. "How do we do?"

"Lucky. Nobody hit. We got between eight and a dozen of 'em cold, I'd say. A number of others'll be nursing various parts for a time. They won't try that again."

McNair punched the empty loads out of his .45, which he, like most of the men, had resorted to in the last frenetic moments when a few Cheyenne had nearly achieved the breastworks.

"John," von Leibnitz said painfully, "let me say that I am sorry. For—I think I am to blame—for Miss Lee going off alone."

McNair lightly rubbed a scorched palm over his sweat-grimed face, slowly shaking his head. "Karl, I just don't know. I don't know where the blame goes."

"They will not come again . . . maybe tonight?"

"Doubt it. Not unless they've an unusually high crop of agnostics in the crowd. The pious ones worry about their spirits wandering forever in darkness—if they're killed by night. . . ."

"Then?"

"Then—" McNair glanced up at the sweep of bright blue sky, where a few mare's-tail clouds made anemic wisps and a single black buzzard hung static-winged. "Unless there's rain, and I don't expect any, our water'll stretch through maybe noon tomorrow. From then on we dehydrate. Till I'd guess about day after tomorrow. In this heat, no longer. Because by then we'll be in no condition to hold off another charge."

McNair pushed laboriously to his feet, intending to make another check of the men. Then he halted in his tracks, glancing at von Leibnitz, keeping his next words too low for the men's ears.

"Unless . . ."

"What?"

"Those mortars," McNair murmured. "Nobody in Spotted Wolf's gang knows how to use one, or we'd know it by now. I just hope to God none of 'em figures it out. Or we won't have even two days. . . ."

Chapter Eighteen

Honus Gant had miscalculated how long it would take him to hit the patrol's trail. He crossed it a full day after he'd expected to. This was at noon. He followed the trail north. At about midafternoon, he picked up a sound of distant shots. He went faster.

An exhausted hour later, he came to where the patrol had run into the ambush. By then, the battle had shifted to the hill, as he could tell from the shooting.

Honus was a little frantic as he went over the ambush site. If Cresta Lee had been with them . . .

With them or not, there was no sign of her hereabout. Just the scalped and arm-severed bodies of five troopers scattered through the brush.

A little more reconnoitering left him anything but reassured. He fervently hoped now that Cresta Lee hadn't found the patrol. For if not among the dead, she faced certain annihilation with the troopers on the hill. And there wasn't a thing Honus Gant could do.

He couldn't get through the Indian lines to join them, and if he struck out for Fort Reunion and help, any reinforcements would arrive much too late.

The only thing left was to work in as close to the Cheyenne camp as possible and see what he could learn.

It took him a full hour of crawling and inching on his belly through deep grass to reach the top of a shallow hillock some two hundred yards to the camp's rear. And by then, with first twilight on the way, it was getting harder to make out individual objects.

He could tell enough. The skin lodges were erected, indicating that the Indians intended to remain where they were until the last Long Knife scalp was theirs. With a certain victory in sight, they were mildly celebrating with a dog feast. A crackle of anticipation mingled with the anguished wailing of Cheyenne women. They must have paid a price, cornering the troops.

Honus took note of other things. Such as the two heavy Studebakers captured by the Indians. These had been lugged into camp and pulled up by the cluster of lodges.

He saw the single prisoner they had taken—a slight, youthful trooper. A lot of the braves wore odds and ends of uniforms, so it was the young fellow's light skin that identified him rather than his dark yellow-piped blouse and yellow-striped sky-blue trousers.

Funny thing. There was no guard on this soldier. He didn't appear to be bound or restrained. Something else was funny. He had no boots. And that ludicrous straw topper was no campaign hat.

Incredulous, Honus blinked against the distance and fading light and peered closer.

Trooper be damned! It was Cresta Lee. . . .

It didn't make a lot of sense, but there she was. The uniform indicated that she must have caught up with the patrol—then had somehow gotten herself captured by the Cheyenne again.

After his first surprise, Honus mulled things over coolly. Two weeks ago, he would have fretted and sweated his way to a proper course of action. Now he sized up the situation at once and did some matter-of-fact thinking.

Cresta Lee first: she seemed to be in no danger at the moment. Apparently, thanks to her former status, she was more a reluctant guest than a prisoner. She was sitting on a pack off to one side, but not far off. If she tried to run or slip away, she'd be quickly seen and easily overhauled.

What about the men trapped on the hill? What could one man out beyond the circling Cheyenne, his presence not suspected, do for them?

Honus' gaze tightened speculatively on the charred half-moon of scorched brush that blackened the lower half of the hill. The Cheyenne had tried the brush fire stunt again, this time in vain.

His glance swiveled gradually to his left, following the line of terrain. He began to smile. Maybe . . .

But what about Cresta? His idea stood a strong chance of throwing the Cheyenne camp into chaos. And just as good a chance of precipitating her death.

No. He couldn't take the risk.

Yet the more he thought about it, the more he thought of how it would give the trapped men a fighting chance.

The answer? Obvious. Get Cresta out of the camp first. Only how in hell did a white man, a gangling, overgrown, naturally clumsy white man, go about getting inside an Indian camp undetected—much less spiriting a girl away from under their noses?

Chewing morosely on the problem, Honus saw a tall warrior with a gorgeous white-feather headdress leave a small group of braves. He walked toward Cresta.

Honus had noticed him before—minutes ago, when he had laid down the law to some bucks who were loud and obstreperous. He had guessed then—and now felt suddenly sure—that this man was Spotted Wolf. . . .

Chapter Nineteen

Dourly studying her ragged fingernails, Cresta Lee glanced up as Spotted Wolf approached her. Then she came to her feet and greeted him.

She respected the war chief. He had treated her well, as well as ever, since her recapture. She knew he could be ruthless, but she had often seen his kindlier side. In some ways, because of their age difference, he had been more a father to her than a husband.

He made the sound of friendliness.

"*Hau-hau*, Brown Hair. We have not had time to talk together. Are you well? Have the women offered you any harm?"

"*Hone-ehe-hemo* knows that since I became his wife, no Cheyenne has treated me badly."

"But you ran away. You brought shame on my lodge."

"I am sorry for this. But my heart was with my people. Even the rites do not change the heart. I was not a Cheyenne."

"Yet I thought you content."

"I wished you to think so."

The faintest of smiles flickered over Spotted Wolf's craggy mouth.

He was a big rugged man, handsome by the standards of any race. His carriage was youthful, and he dressed as his braves, in the summer costume of breechcloth and leggings. His hair was braided in the old-fashioned style, hanging in a single glossy coil across his right shoulder. Little devil's horns of white touched the black hair of his temples, and they seemed to bristle in his anger.

"You are clever, Brown Hair. But I knew this. Do you understand? It was not the public shame. It was the thing between us. I trusted you."

"I say again that I am sorry. But it is as I said. Will Spotted Wolf send me to the burning pole for his pride?"

He frowned. "Do you think that I would hurt you, Brown Hair?"

"How could I tell? Spotted Wolf can be terrible in his anger."

"But never toward you. No. You have brought me pain; it is not the other way. Here." He brought his fist to his heart.

"It has brought me pain too. Spotted Wolf knows that I do not lie."

"Never with your lips, Brown Hair. Are you sure that you don't know how the small cannon in that wagon are used?"

"I have told you I do not."

Nor did she, but she would have lied about that. She knew why he wanted to solve the workings of the mortars. Then she noted the grim humor in his face; he was having a little joke. She grinned with an effort.

Suddenly a sentry came running from the far side of the camp. He crossed directly over to Spotted Wolf and spoke rapidly. One was coming alone from the southeast—a *veho*, white man. He was leading mules.

Spotted Wolf went to see for himself.

Cresta seated herself on the pack again. Her eyes restlessly studied the camp. The twilight was scaling down to a dull glow. It would be full dusk before long. She was close to the edge of the camp, and it took all her will power not to seize her opportunity and make a dash for freedom. But she knew that the Cheyenne nearby were watching her, even when they appeared not to be.

Noises of excitement began churning this way from the camp's south end. Then Spotted Wolf came striding back, a whole drove of women, children and yapping feists crowding behind. They surrounded a squat ape of a white man who walked with a quick rolling step.

It was Isaac Q. Cumber. He was leading his saddle horse and six mules laden with bulky pack tarps. Cresta's heart sank. Von Leibnitz' courier must have reached Colonel Tabler too late. Even if the colonel had sent troops after Cumber, he'd obviously managed to elude them.

He spotted Cresta.

"Lord declare. Hoddy, little lady. Just couldn't keep away from the Injuns, hey? Heh heh."

"*Veho Pavhetan* comes late to our lodges," Spotted Wolf said coldly.

"Yeh." Cumber slacked down on a pack and took off his hat, sleeving his sweaty forehead. "Couldn't be helped none." He tipped his burrlike head toward Cresta. "You c'n ask that 'un about it. Her and her sojer boy throwed a wrench in the works."

He told pungently of how Honus and Cresta had destroyed his wagon and the guns. Of being forced to return to Fort Reunion and then riding posthaste to Cheyenne where he knew that a freighter friend of his had a fresh consignment of Winchesters in his warehouse and was willing to part with them for cash, no questions asked.

"Took ever' cent I had left in my poke," Cumber said aggrievedly. "Tell you, Wolf, it's a caution what-all a man'll sacrifice fer his Cheyenne friends."

Spotted Wolf gave a short laugh and said something in his own tongue.

Cumber chuckled uneasily. "What's 'at, Wolf?"

"He says that's a lot of buffalo chips," Cresta translated, not too loosely.

"Thought that's what he said," Cumber muttered.

"Well, Brown Hair," Spotted Wolf said in his precise, careful mission English, "it seems there's a thing or two you have failed to mention."

"Oh, well," Cresta said. "It's all coming back now."

By this time nearly everybody in camp had gathered around. The braves were hungrily eying the pack mules. At a nod from Spotted Wolf, they surged around the mules, slashing the diamond hitches and dragging the heavy tarps to the ground. Warriors dropped their old muskets to seize up new repeaters and examine them lovingly. What a thing to see a whole dozen *Mila Hanska* across one of these! . . .

Cresta watched the warriors, but kept her attention on the exchange between Spotted Wolf and Cumber. Yes, Spotted Wolf said, the Army paychest would go to *Veho Pavhetan* as promised, though he was late bringing the guns. So late that Spotted Wolf had been unable to hold back his young men any longer.

When the scouts had brought word of a Long Knife patrol deep in Spotted Wolf's territory, he had been forced to yield to the young braves and lead them in pursuit of the pony soldiers, though less than half his men were as yet armed with the new rifles. He had left a few older men to wait at the rendezvous so that if *Veho Pavhetan* still came, they could direct him to wherever the band was.

"Had to travel by night, y'understand," Cumber said toothily. "Better late'n never, Wolf."

"Yes, Cumber, but your lateness has caused young men to die who might be alive to fight some more. Look. See on the hill?"

"Smoke. Seen it a-riding in. So you druv 'em up on that roost, hey?"

"For two days we followed them. We spied on their camps at night. Last night, when Brown Hair left the soldiers' camp, my scouts seized her. Today we attacked. But it was too soon; the thing went badly. We will still get them all, but it will take time. Another day, maybe two. And now that you've brought the guns, my young men will be impatient to try them. Too many have already died charging the hill. If they will not wait . . ."

"Yep. I savvy that. You got something in mind, Wolf?"

"Come with me."

Cresta watched obliquely as the two went over to the mortar wagon. Cumber had his look, and she saw him grin and turn to Spotted Wolf, nodding vigorously. She caught most of the talk that followed, enough to gather that Cumber knew how to load and aim and fire a mortar but that it was getting too dark to aim one with any accuracy. They must wait for the first light of dawn. Then Wolf would see what these dandy little popguns could do. Yes, sir. Lord declare.

Right now, if his old friend Wolf would give him the loan of a few braves, they could get these here mortars moved into position at the foot of the hill.

"And what does Good White Man ask for this favor?" Spotted Wolf said the trader's Cheyenne name in English, giving the words a bright-edged contempt.

"Heh heh. Well, the paychest naturally. Then you and your boys take me 'n' it safe down to Mexico—but right to where I say."

"Done." Spotted Wolf ignored Cumber's outstretched hand and called to some braves who were idling around. He told them to give *Veho Payhetan* a hand. Then he came back to Cresta.

"Follow me, Brown Hair."

She fell in behind him like an obedient wife. Spotted Wolf led the way to a weathered old lodge that she recognized: its scraped hide surface was painted with mystic symbols. It housed old Sweet Teal, the wise woman.

Spotted Wolf thrust aside the deerskin over the entrance and ducked inside. A very old Cheyenne woman, toothless and yellow-skinned, crouched over rows of brightly colored pebbles that were spread on the ground in intricate designs.

"*Aie! Aie!*" She stabbed a bony finger at Cresta. "It is her! The white one! It is even as I said, and she has returned. *Heyoka!* Fool, did I not tell you your fate is written in her evil star?"

"*Nenana onohistahe,*" Spotted Wolf said irritably. "Shut your mouth, Mother. Down on your face, Brown Hair. . . ."

He bound her hands and feet with flinty strands of thong.

That, Cresta thought bleakly, cut off any possibility of her stealing out of the camp after full dark.

"*Veho Payhetan* will show me how to use the small cannon. You will watch her till I return, Mother."

"*Hau!*" whispered old Sweet Teal. "The white one has put a spell on your brain. Beware of her, *heyoka!* See, this bright stone is my *hmunha*. Strong medicine! I have cut my hand on its edge, and in my blood it is written—beware! I see black blood and death. Take your knife, *Hone-ehe-hemo*, and run it into her white-eyed heart. Now, before—"

"*Hekotosz!* I told you to shut up. Hear me, Mother. If she is harmed, I will have your wrinkled hide for patching on old moccasins. Do not forget."

With a lithe motion he stooped through the doorway and was gone. Old Sweet Teal pored over her stones. She drooled weird curses, and did not look at the girl.

Cresta was lying on a heap of soft pelts. With an effort she rolled onto her side, easing her position. She peered about the small frugally furnished house of hide. She coughed. The fire in the central firetrench was smoking, and the tipi's smokehole was drawing badly. The light flickered on the old crone's withered face, a crusty yellow mask except for her thin moving lips.

What a pickle, Cresta thought disgustedly. What had happened to all her precious practicality? If you could improve your lot, do so; otherwise make the best of it. She'd followed the first guideline with Johnny McNair, the second with Spotted Wolf.

Now she had broken the pattern. And look what had happened. Well . . . she had no one but herself to blame. Running off in the night on a whim, like some half-baked schoolgirl. Straight back into Spotted Wolf's arms.

And for what, for God's sake! Honus Gant—who couldn't give less of a damn what anyone did for him, so long as the causes of Right and Virtue were served. Lordy. With all the other uncertainties that had been plaguing her, you'd think she'd have had the sense . . .

With no warning, the two parts ran together in her mind,

sending a panicky shock clear to her toes. Uncertainties! Johnny McNair! Honus Gant! . . .

Honus! That stubborn, stuffy, red-haired, red-eared, red-necked farmboy-at-heart!

Sudden tears stung Cresta's eyes. Oh—what kind of a fool was she? If she *had* to fall in love, why not with Johnny McNair? Why with a lanky, homely recruit with nothing but his scrimped Army savings to his name and no higher ambition than being a dirt farmer back in Ohio?

And why, above all, couldn't she have admitted it before now? Now, when it was much too late . . .

Old Sweet Teal scattered the stones with an angry sweep of her skinny hand. Mumbling, she got on her hands and knees and groped beneath her buffalo hide pallet. She pulled out a square-faced gin bottle. Uncorking it, she took a long professional pull. Big *hmunha*, Cresta thought.

She eased herself against a willow backrest and glared balefully at Cresta Lee.

"Fools fools fools," she chanted toothlessly. "All *heyoka*. Fools. I know. *Aie*, I know. I read your evil star, white one. Blood! Blood of Spotted Wolf!"

Again she fumbled beneath the pallet. This time she drew forth a bit of whetstone and a long skinning knife worn thin as an icicle. She began to sharpen the blade with slow spare over-and-under strokes. Occasionally she took another nip from the bottle.

Her redstone eyes glittered rheumily. She never took them off the white girl.

Chapter Twenty

Honus felt uneasy as he watched Cresta follow Spotted Wolf to a small tipi that was set off somewhat from the others. But it was only a few minutes before the war chief emerged, closed the skin flap over the firelit entrance and headed away across the camp.

Honus was relieved. But not very.

He had seen Cumber ride in. He had watched the braves unload the mortars at the trader's direction and carry them toward the foot of the slope. By then it was too dark to make out anything more.

Honus didn't know much about the mortars. He had watched an artillery unit at Jefferson Barracks practice with the deadly little gadgets and had an idea what they were capable of.

He ran his eye over the camp again. Scrub oak patches here and there. Tipis. Fires. Orange scallops of firelight glimmering on rough blackness of the stream.

The stream. The tipi where Cresta was had been pitched only a few yards from its bank. And the banks were clotted with masses of willow and oak thickets at that point. . . .

Honus slithered back off his grassy rise, got to his feet and cut away to his right, crutching furiously along through the darkness. Ahead he saw an oily frosting of starlight on water.

This was the creek about a hundred yards below the camp.

Honus climbed down the bank and paused to cache his Winchester and his crutch under a matting of dry grass. They would be bulky nuisances, and he could get along without a crutch if he remembered not to throw his full weight on his nearly healed leg.

He waded into the water, feeling the chilly clutch of the current at his legs. He was surprised to find that the water was hip-deep, but all the better. Its quick gurgling was a soft cover for the small noises he made slogging slowly upstream between the willow-choked banks.

The stream made a deep bend before it passed through the Cheyenne encampment. As he moved into the outflung shimmer of firelight, Honus sank down to his chin and hugged the left bank. Awkwardly stabbing his good leg against the clutching muck, he struck into the heart of the camp.

He didn't have to lift up, even if he'd dared, to get a picture of his surroundings. He was plied from every side by a rich cacophony of noises: explosions of talk, laughter, the high-pitched wailing of the bereaved women. He smelled food cooking; dappled firelight and shadow played through the masking brush.

Twigs crackled. Honus shrank against a drooping mass of willow fronds. Four yards upstream a woman came down the bank, knelt and dipped a skin waterbag. It seemed to him that it took ages for the bag to fill. Cold cramps locked his muscles. When she finally left the streamside, he had to squeeze out a conscious effort to get his limbs in motion again.

He had marked in his mind the exact appearance of the bank and foliage behind the lodge. But from the stream, everything looked different. Well, he was about the right distance inside the camp, and this looked like it. . . .

Dragging himself slowly from the water, Honus inched forward on his belly, pulling himself along by hooking in elbows and knees, going up the bank between the willow stems. Leaves whispered along his head and sides. Gently poking aside a few branches, he saw the small tipi not twenty feet away.

Thank God it was isolated from the other lodges and none of the Cheyenne had congregated on either side of the stream at this point. Flattened on his belly again, Honus wormed out of the brush into fairly deep grass. His chest scraped dew and damp earth; his mind swung unreasonably to the thought of snakes. Rattlers in particular, but snakes. Did they like cool grass? . . .

He stopped a couple of yards short of the lodge and fumbled out his sheath knife. Not only was Cresta Lee probably tied up, he might have to cut through the tipi wall.

In the same moment an oddly susurrated sound, like a low inarticulate mumbling, reached him. The voice came unmistakably from the tipi, and it sounded like a very old, very sick or very intoxicated woman. Not Cresta Lee for sure.

Honus froze. What rotten luck! It hadn't even occurred to him that she might not be alone. A few moments ago his teeth had been chattering with cold. Now he could feel his wet clothes warming with his sweaty vapors.

Well, what did he do now? Stay where he was—wait? Back up? Or just what?

The woman's voice began to rise with a kind of atonal fury, till it turned cracking and high-pitched. Then he heard Cresta give a sharp answer—apparently in Cheyenne. The woman shrilled back at her. There was a soft bump and rustle, as if of a struggle.

Honus quickly covered the remaining distance and yanked at the deerskin cover. It pulled up far enough for him to jam his head and shoulders under. He saw an old woman on her hands and knees, her back to him, stabbing feebly at Cresta Lee with a long thin knife. The girl lay on her side, hands tied at her back and her tied legs doubled up, jabbing with her feet. Quick as a cat, she was managing to ward off the old woman, who kept giving low sickly groans between her bursts of shrill diatribe.

With a cry she tried to smother Cresta with her frail weight, at the same time drawing the knife back for a sweeping cut. Honus squirmed wildly under the tipi wall and lunged at the old woman's back.

At the same time she gurgled gently and slumped across Cresta Lee like a tired child, the knife slipping from her fingers. Honus dragged her aside.

For once Cresta Lee was speechless. She simply stared at him. While she stared, Honus picked up the knife and cut away her ropes, muttering, "Guess she won't raise an alarm for a while. She seems to be sick—"

"She's drunk."

Cresta rolled to her feet and crouched on her heels, rubbing her wrists, eying him incredulously. "My God! I can't believe it."

"What can't you?"

"Oh, forget it. How did you get here?"

"Waded in by the creek. And we'd better be leaving now, the same way—"

"Wait a minute."

Her dark gaze snapped onto a heap of heterogeneous gear. Scrambling over to it, she pulled out what looked like an army blanket tied around some other things.

"I thought so. The stuff I had. The old thief! All right. Lead the way. . . ."

Honus ducked his head out under the pegged-down cover where he'd entered, peered around and slithered out. He elbowed and kneed his gangling way through the wet grass into the brush and down to the water. Cresta moved right behind him in quick graceful silence, hissing at him not to make so damned much noise.

Once they were in the water, he had the better of it. She was so short that several times the deep current nearly swept her off her feet. He steadied her with an arm.

By the time they were well around the bend and the camp was cut off, it was a different story. Honus could feel a rubbery weakness attacking his muscles. The cold was getting to him fast; he was hardly able to pull himself up the bank.

"You ill, Buster?"

"No," Honus chattered. He felt under the dry grass where he

had left his rifle and crutch, got them, and eased shakingly to his feet. "Now, the first thing, we have to—"

"The first thing, how long since you've eaten?"

"That's not important. Those men up there need our help!"

"Well, fine, Buster. But just now you couldn't help a drowning gnat. Look at you. And don't tell me you don't need a couple hours' rest and something to eat. Come on. . . ."

Honus knew when not to argue. He was literally trembling with weakness and dizzy from hunger. He had stretched his final rations impossibly thin, and the last mouthful had gone down twenty-four hours ago. Docilely he followed Cresta Lee across the thick-grassed prairie, heading away from the camp.

She found a sheltered place on the side of a long knoll, a nook formed by a weathered sandstone outcrop. The rock was still warm from the day's heat. He sank gratefully against it and let his muscles go loose, and shut his eyes.

Cresta scrunched down beside him. She untied her bundle and spread the blanket out. "The devil!"

He opened his eyes, peering at her in the starshine. She was holding up an Army .45. "Look. Yours. That damned old thief! She took everything I had."

Honus eyed the blanket and food and medicine. "Where did you get it all?"

She sawed off a piece of raw bacon and stuck it in her mouth, and chewed judiciously. "Stole it."

Honus discovered that even bad issue bacon and flinty lumps of hardtack were manna when you were half-starved.

Cresta was curious. "How'd you find your way here, anyhow? I'd have thought you'd lose yourself inside a mile of the cave."

"In spite of your overwhelming confidence," he muttered, "I managed to make it."

"Oh, don't be so damned touchy."

It all sounded pretty much as usual, and Honus had the feeling that a dislocated part of his world had jigsawed back into place. He told her about his encounter with the Indian family and of getting both food and directions—"otherwise I'd never have made it, if that gives you any satisfaction."

Cresta told him of her experiences since leaving him. At least as much as she chose to tell. Honus had a feeling of gaps in her story.

"What about those mortars?" he said. "I didn't think Cumber would use them tonight."

"He's just setting them up, he said. At dawn . . ."

Honus gnawed the fatty bacon and muttered, "If he can place just one shell on that hilltop, it'll send your lieutenant and his men to kingdom come."

She moved a little: he became suddenly conscious of her friendly shoulder and curving closeness of thigh. "Well . . . dammit, what can we do?"

"I have a kind of idea. . . ."

He chewed more slowly. His thoughts, suddenly, refused to hold to either ideas or food. His mind was full of her, of the molding tightness of her shoulder and thigh and, hardly seen in dim starlight and black shadow yet so well known, the cherished image of that proud, sad, scornful, lovely face.

Desire rushed through him like a prairie fire. He shook like a leaf. Even in the relative incongruity of the moment, he couldn't stop himself. He let the food drop from his hands and rolled sideways and grabbed her.

She fought him—"*No!* What are you—? Stop it! *Honus!*"—but for only a few seconds. Then her body relaxed into the hollowed rock and her arms slipped up and pulled him tighter into the sweet and vibrant crush of her mouth.

He didn't know how long it lasted. Then he felt the half-panicked twist of her lithe body: she broke free enough to give him a hard palm-flat clout across the jaw. It jarred him back on his side. She sat up, glaring at him.

"No! No more of that, d'you understand?"

Honus rubbed his jaw reproachfully. "You liked it."

"What's *that* got to do with it? It doesn't matter whether or not I liked it! That has nothing at all to do with it! Don't you dare do that again, Honus Gant!"

Her voice was trembling, and he realized how much his stupidity had upset her. He stared disconsolately at his big hands. Why had he been such a fool?

"We're a man and woman alone, that's all. That's all there is to it," she went on in a voice of quiet fury. "We're different, you and I—too different for it to be anything else. And don't pretend otherwise!"

"I'm not," he said wearily. "Do you want to hear the plan?"

"Go ahead with it. Just see that you keep your distance, boy."

Chapter Twenty-one

From where Honus lay in the grass behind the screening brush, he could see the low dance of flames through a filigree of twigs. He could hear the voices of the Cheyenne men and women and children working along the line of south-eating fire, beating at it with hides and blankets.

His heart sank as he watched. They were defeating the blaze without too much sweat. If only the wind would rise! It had been sporadic for hours, and the tiny fanning blaze that held now wasn't enough to sweep the flames into the unstoppable holocaust that a prairie fire could easily become. . . .

Honus' gaze shifted to the tall form of the sentry who was patrolling the pony picket line. The Cheyenne had halted not over thirty feet from where Honus lay concealed. He had his head turned to watch the fire and the beaters, who were several hundred yards off to his left.

You could still take him, Honus thought. *Now's the time. Even you couldn't miss.*

Only what was the good? Unless the fire did its share of the job, running the horses off would hardly finish it. . . .

He and Cresta Lee had built up a good-sized fire on the flank of the steep knoll, the side facing away from the camp. Armed with a half-dozen burning brands apiece, they had worked in opposite directions, running along a rough line north of the camp and flinging their torches into brush and deep patches of sun-dried grass. Unlike the vegetation on the hill, it was like a tinderbox.

Honus had then told Cresta Lee in no uncertain terms to get out of sight and stay there while he put phase two of the scheme into operation.

Widely circling the camp at a run, he'd come up on its south side, where he'd taken to the creek again. This time he was wading upstream, armed with Winchester and .45, holding both above the water.

Cresta had told him the Cheyenne ponies were tethered behind the camp on a rope strung between two cottonwoods on the stream's bank where the deep lush grass was still green. There'd be a guard, she had warned him. As before, his approach by the noisy stream had let Honus steal in close—almost to the edge of the picket line. All he'd had to do was lift himself out of the water.

The fires they'd set had quickly exploded into flaming masses of brush and grass before the beaters got to them. But in a few minutes the fire had been slowed along its whole perimeter by belts of sparser growth. And by now the beaters, forming a line between the flames and their camp, had it pretty well under control. . . .

There!

Honus stiffened with exultation. The wind was coming up strongly again, flattening the grasses like a great cool hand. The ponies whickered and stamped restlessly. Wind scooped the flames high in tattered yellow corkscrews. And now the faint cries of the beaters took on a note of panic.

Let it keep up this way for just ten minutes and they'd be forced to abandon their camp. Now was Honus' moment to abet the confusion.

Carefully he drew the ready-cocked Winchester up to his shoulder and took aim on the sentry's motionless figure. He pressed the trigger.

Dampness, a misfire, a jammed cartridge, whatever it was—there was a futile snap.

The sentry turned his head instantly. He stared straight at Honus' hiding place, listening. Honus hugged the earth, his heart pounding. Abruptly the sentry heeled around and pointed his rifle at the brush.

"Niva tato?"

When no answer was forthcoming, he light-footed forward to have a look.

This was it, Honus thought. All the Cheyenne had to do was beat the bushes. And being caught flat on his belly would be fatal. His pistol was jammed into his holster and flapped down. . . .

Honus sprang to his feet, whirling his rifle about his head. He lunged at his enemy, at the same time letting go with a grandiose whoop intended to disconcert him.

It was enough to send the nervous ponies into paroxysms of total panic. They struck out with their hoofs and tore at the picket rope. This, more than the noise itself, made the sentry miss.

He fired hastily at Honus from the hip, then leaped aside to avoid the surge of rearing, plunging ponies as they piled against the straining rope.

The Cheyenne had no time to lever and fire again. Just time enough to club his own rifle and meet the white man's driving attack. They swung at the same time, the steel barrels ringing together. The shock of it numbed Honus' wrists; that and the solid impact tore the Winchester from his hands.

He flung himself heavily against the Cheyenne, locking a hand around his rifle and grappling him to immobilize the weapon. The brave tried to jerk the rifle free. He failed, then suddenly let go of it and whipped his knife from its sheath.

Honus felt rather than saw the movement: he leaped back, holding the rifle awkwardly across his body with both hands. The Cheyenne sliced savagely at his head and missed by an inch or so.

Dropping the rifle, Honus grabbed at the Indian's knife

wrist. He got it, but the Cheyenne promptly hooked a foot behind his heel and tripped him, then fell with him.

Honus, the Indian on top, lit on his back with a hard-driven grunt. He felt the squirming power of his adversary's slick near-naked body. He clung with both hands to the sentry's right wrist. Then gave up half his hold to snake his right hand to his holster flap and tug his pistol free, cocking it just as the Cheyenne seized his arm.

"*Veho!*" the Indian snarled. "*Katam, evetazistov!*" as he threw the strength of his right shoulder and arm into forcing the knife downward toward Honus' throat. Inch by inch.

Honus felt his left hand losing its sweaty grip. The tip of the blade was poised three inches from his Adam's apple.

With a supreme desperation he put all the fury of his tough young muscles into two efforts: halting the knife's descent and twisting the pistol muzzle upward.

A hoarse cry left the Indian. He knew he was losing. Then the pistol thundered against his ribs, and he had lost. His tight-strung body slumped across Honus, and the strength ran out of him.

Honus rolled him aside and scrambled to his feet. He nearly cried out at the pain shooting through his leg. It wasn't ready for the punishment of hard exertion.

The wind was still gusting strongly, out of the beaters' control now. He could see their dark running forms against the flames as they retreated toward the camp to throw their belongings hastily together. In a minute some would be hurrying this way to fetch their mounts.

Honus ran over to the picket line.

Not all the ponies had panicked. A number only shifted tranquilly to the surgings of their fellows. A shaggy little pinto pricked up its ears and whickered at him. He peered closer—a brandmark was etched blackly clear on the pinto's hip. He'd been stolen or traded from a white man, and the brand was a fairly recent one. The pony stretched out a friendly, inquisitive muzzle.

"I think you and I can make it together," Honus murmured. "Hold still. Good boy."

He grasped the horsehair rein and ducked under the picket rope and swung up on the pony's back in one awkward lunge, as he'd used to mount old Bruno, Aunt Maddie's shay horse. It was a cinch.

He pulled his knife and reached down and sawed the picket line in two, then pulled his mount away and around. He was delighted with its response to a touch of his heel. A trained cowpony! Nothing would suit his purpose better.

Despite the slack picket line, the ponies were slow to grasp the fact of their freedom, milling aimlessly, rubbing and ramming at one another. *No animal dumber than a horse,* N Troop's O'Hearn used to say. *Do his thinking for him.*

Honus kneed his animal into a quick back-forth trot, keeping the loose mass of ponies between himself and the camp. He could tell from the shouting that some of the Cheyenne were running this way now. As yet they hadn't picked him out against the darkness, but they could tell that something was wrong with the pony herd.

Honus yelled and hoorawed, swinging his mount in and out against the confused animals. They started to shuffle away from him: their confusion found direction. He pushed them harder, pointing them as well as he could toward the Cheyenne lodges.

Somebody fired off a rifle: maybe they had spotted him. Whatever the reason, it was the spark needed to whack the slow-drifting animals into a sudden bolting. They poured away like a released arrow. Straight for the camp.

Honus flattened to his pony's withers. He clamped his knees and held for dear life, the pinto's muscles bunching and churning under him as he stretched after them, yelling at the top of his cracking voice.

He had firelit glimpses of Indians scattering to left and right as the *remuda* hit the edge of the camp. They swept across it and thundered on, cutting away west out of the path of the advancing grass fire. Lodges were hammered flat, fires pounded

177

to memories of drifting ash. A bedlam of shrieks and shouts reigned on every side as the camp splintered into utter chaos, most of it obscured by the bronze haze of stampede dust rolling against the firelight.

Injuns ain't hardly never caught off guard, Honus remembered his friend the old scout saying. So that on those few occasions they were, their lack of the white military's discipline generally threw them into complete rout.

That recalled bit of lore was the key to Honus' plan. That— and the hope that the troopers on the hill would be alert enough to seize advantage of the distraction.

Honus, hanging in the herd's wake, veered his mount hard to the right now. He was thinking of Cumber and those mortars. He sent the pinto crashing through the chaparral tangles toward the base of the promontory.

Suddenly a flash and roar.

A mortar shell climbed invisibly into the night in a long screaming arc. It exploded below the hill's crown. A jarring sear of light bathed the whole scape.

The shell had fallen short. But it was obvious that—as he'd feared—Cumber, alarmed by the fire and the stampede, wasn't waiting for dawn to set off a mortar barrage. A difference of minute correction in his aim—and he might drop the next one right in the middle of the troopers.

Flamelight pierced the masses of thicket ahead of Honus. He bolted suddenly through the raking brush and came out clear of it.

The clearing was lit by a tall fire. It played bronze glints off the three mortars set in a precise line. Cumber was tugging frenziedly at one of them, savagely cursing as he edged it around to a slightly altered facing. Ordinarily it took two men to carry one of the weapons by the handles sunk in the mounting block. . . .

Even as Honus burst into the clearing, he heard the faint bark of an officer's voice yelling orders on the hill's summit. In a moment the troopers would be boiling down across the rim in a full charge. The tide of battle would swing on a hair now. If that second mortar were brought into play—!

Honus careened his mount to a stop, yanking at his .45. He'd forgotten how it always jammed in the stiff leather. He needed both hands to free it. Now, needing to keep one hand to the reins, he jerked wildly at the gun one-handed.

Cumber straighted around, squat and swift, his small vicious elf's face puckered with fury. Then he darted for the Sharps leaning against a mortar block three yards away.

Honus let go of his reins to free both hands for his gun. It came suddenly free. He'd unintentionally cocked the weapon while yanking at it, and now just as inadvertently pressed the trigger and came within an ace of blowing off his right foot.

Cumber whipped up his rifle. His shot seared the pinto. It reared precariously high. Honus, scrabbling wildly at the air, was slid off the pony's glossy rump slick as a flapjack off a seasoned griddle.

His bad leg was doubled under him as he hit the stony ground. Even as he crashed helplessly on his side—the scene before him dissolving in an explosion of scarlet agony—he knew that he'd split the nearly healed thigh open again. . . .

He clutched the leg with both hands, feeling the hot slippery bloodflow. He heard his own voice yelling as he rolled arch-backed in a twisting surge of pain off the hurt limb. He saw Cumber through a pink fog. But the trader was not even looking at him. His head was turned, all his attention on the lifting racket of the cavalrymen charging down the hill.

He flung the rifle aside and leaped back to the second mortar. He worked furiously to haul it still farther around.

Honus had lost his pistol. It had bounded out of his hand. He fought the waves of blinding pain to focus his eyes, wildly searching the ground. He saw the steely wink of gunmetal in the firelight some ten feet away. . . .

He heaved onto his chest and belly and dragged his body forward in spasmodic lurches, trying to ignore the pain that grunted from his throat with every movement.

Sickness surged into his mouth. He was afraid of passing

out before he reached the gun—and nearly did. He scooped it painfully into his fist and braced his elbow in the gravel and tried to steady Cumber's wavering form in his sights. His hand was wobbling impossibly.

He fired. The slug whined off the mortar. Cumber jerked his sooty red-eyed face around. The face split in a laugh. The mortar went off.

The roar of it mingled with Honus' next shot. Cumber's body jerked. Honus heard the shell whistle against blackness as a peppering of shots across the encampment told of the troopers' arrival.

Honus blinked against powdersmoke and pain. Dimly, as his senses raged away in a faint, he saw Cumber going up on his toes in a slow sinewy pirouette and then collapsing across the mortar. . . .

Chapter Twenty-two

Tendrils of ash puffed under Cresta's moccasins as she walked up the scorched bank from the creek, soap and towel in hand, fluffing out her wet hair. The violet dawn lay bleak on the baked prairie. And on her mood.

She walked back toward the camp, not even glancing off to her right at the Cheyennes who had survived last night's engagement. The wailing of the women had ebbed away toward morning. The remainder of Spotted Wolf's band, old and young, sat huddled and silent among the belongings they had salvaged from their burned-over camp. A dozen or so troopers stood off a ways, rifles slung under their arms, keeping a casual watch.

The engagement had been short and swift. Spotted Wolf, in the act of trying to rally his confused warriors, had been killed by an Army bullet. His death had left them all stunned and apathetic. An Army patrol of one third the Cheyennes' numbers would have no problems herding them to Darlington and the agency.

The troopers were breakfasting as Cresta walked back through the bivouac. She returned to the hospital area where she had spent most of last night helping Trooper Robbins with the wounded.

Lieutenant von Leibnitz lay in the shade of the mortar wagon, his back propped against a pack. He had a little of his Teutonic color back. Cresta went by him without so much as a glance. Then she halted, biting her lip, and walked back to him.

"You need anything?" she asked coldly.

"No, nothing. Thank you." He harrumphed with a clear embarrassment. "You say this poultice you put on my wound is something the Indians make?"

"That's what I said."

Von Leibnitz gazed across the rolls of tawny buffalo grass shimmering in the morning light. "This is a big land," he murmured. "A very hard land. I think it will take more than—how do you call them?—milk-and-molasses frumps to settle such a country. It will take the strong. Strong American women such as you."

Cresta said nothing.

He cleared his throat. "What I try to say, Miss Lee, is that you are a remarkable young woman. And if a stiff-necked fool like me can be made to see this, so can you make others see it. Do you understand?"

As she walked slowly on to the other wagon, Cresta was scowling. In his awkward way, von Leibnitz had handed her a carte blanche of entry into the clannish world of the career officer: it knocked any practical reservations she might have had about an Army marriage into a cocked hat. Why didn't it mean a damned thing?

The rear pucker of the supply wagon was open, and she clambered up and stepped inside.

Honus had been made comfortable in the wagon bed, on a heap of blankets donated by some troopers. There were other wounded too, but Honus was the hero of the day to everyone—even Lieutenant McNair, who had insisted on his occupying the relative comfort of the wagon.

She'd never seen a man accept a special privilege with less grace. Even weak and feverish, Honus had gotten unwontedly loud with embarrassed (and embarrassing) objections. He was quiet enough now; he looked rested.

She examined the fresh poultice on his leg, uncomfortably aware of his eyes never leaving her face. "You split this open once more," she said, "and I'll let you bleed to death."

McNair came to the rear pucker and folded his arms on the tailboard, peering in. "Ah. Morning, Gant. How do you feel?"

"Just wonderful," Honus said, "sir."

McNair laughed. "I'll bet. We'll be on the move in an hour or so, taking the captives down to Darlington. You and other wounded'll stay encamped here till you're well enough to ride to Fort Reunion . . . with enough able-bodied men left here to handle your needs."

As he talked, he eyed Honus with that same air of faint astonishment he'd shown since their meeting. Honus, Cresta had noticed, had been trying not very successfully to cover a similar reaction. She knew that she was tied in firmly and irrevocably with whatever impressions these two men had formed of one another. Caught in the middle. She felt irritated and embarrassed—and a little smug, which irritated her even more.

"I've heard a good deal about you, Gant," McNair said in a friendly voice. "We'll have to have a talk sometime."

"Likewise," Honus said, a little ambiguously, "sir."

"Some breakfast, Cresta? Good. Join me when you're ready."

McNair strode away. Cresta covered Honus' leg again, her cheeks flaming. Damn them! What did they mean, anyway? Talk about what?

"He's shorter than I am, some," Honus said thoughtfully.

"What of it, for God's sake?"

"You said he was twice my size."

"Mentally," she snapped, "he is."

She immediately regretted the words. They weren't true, and there was no call for them.

"At midnight," Honus muttered, "your coach will turn into a pumpkin."

"What!"

"Nothing. Nothing at all."

"Oh, I heard you! That was a rotten thing to say. And so damned typical of you, Honus Gant!"

"Look," he said in a low, dogged voice, "it's just honest. From everything you've said, love doesn't enter in at all. You're marrying a man for every wrong reason. . . ."

"I call self-respect a damned good reason!"

Slowly and soberly, Honus shook his head. "Poor Cresta."

That really got her hackles up. "What d'you mean, 'poor Cresta'?"

"I mean that self-respect isn't something you marry into."

"Oh, I know what self-respect is," she gibed savagely. "Hell, yes! It's a li'l ole dirt farm back in Ohio!"

Honus shook his head wearily. "All I'm saying is that you can't run away to it. Self-respect has nothing to do with what others think of you. If you have it, it's there whether or not a single other soul knows about it. Funny."

"What is?"

"Why, that somebody as independent as you wouldn't know that for herself."

He watched her steadily. She dropped her gaze nervously to her hands. Damn! What *was* it? Being kissed by Johnny Mc-Nair was pleasant. Very pleasant indeed. But by now all this damned homely farmboy had to do was *look* at her in a certain way and she could feel the shock of it clear to her toes. As for that passionate moment on the knoll behind the Cheyenne camp, she hadn't even dared dwell on it.

"Cresta . . ."

"What?" She knew well enough what: her lips were trembling and her lashes growing wet.

"I'm sorry. I didn't mean to hurt your feelings."

"My *feelings*!" She got furiously to her feet, banging her head on one of the cover hoops. "Ow! Damn you! My *feelings*!"

She whirled around and climbed over the tailgate and dropped to the ground. She stalked blindly away from the wagon and halted at the edge of the bivouac. Shakingly she dried her eyes. Oh, that *fool!*

She had left her emotions slip momentarily out of control. It wouldn't happen again, ever.

All right. She could not deny what she felt. But she would get over it. She had to. Nothing, by God, *nothing* was going to interfere with the future she had planned so long ago and had suffered through so much to achieve.

She drew her shoulders up and made sure of her composure. She was completely cool as she walked back to join McNair for breakfast.

Some of the troopers close by may have noticed her agitation. McNair hadn't. He had been down by the creek filling his coffeepot. Now he joined her by the fire he'd built; the two of them put together a breakfast of sorts.

His manner had been oddly reserved since their reunion last night. She knew what was troubling him. Knew too that it was up to her, not him, to say something. But for the life of her, she couldn't. So a polite silence held through breakfast.

Finally, frowning into his coffee cup, McNair came abruptly out with it: "Cresta—why did you break your promise?"

"It was a wrong promise to begin with, Johnny. I never should have made it."

"Right or wrong, you broke it."

"Yes." She sat cross-legged facing him. She sipped her coffee and set the cup down by her knee and looked him straight in the eyes. "It won't work, will it?"

The words had sprung to her lips so easily and naturally that Cresta blinked now. Momentarily she was consternated. Had *she* said that?

McNair was silent for a bitterly considering moment. Then he shook his head. "If it were only the other things. But now there's Gant."

Cresta didn't answer at once: she was trying to bring order to her scrambled thoughts. She had worked half a lifetime to build this edifice . . . and only a few minutes ago had renewed it with the coldest of resolutions. Now, in five unexpected words, she had pulled the whole structure down on her head.

And—strangest of all—it had fallen lightly as a feather.

"A blind man couldn't miss it," McNair went on quietly. "You and Gant are as tense with each other as a pair of cats. Yet since last night, you've spent more time with him than the rest of us put together. There are a few other wounded men around, you know." He sighed. "I guess my pride could swallow anything but that. Every time I touched you, there'd be the other man. It would be him, not me, touching you. I'd know it and I'd think of it, always. Finally . . ."

Cresta gave a half-absent nod. A lot of things were coming together at once. And with them, a picture of the whole truth, flooding her consciousness as gently as a spring rain, painlessly and yet with a wrench of sadness, a sense of half-loss.

She had lived with it for so long, the veneer of ambition, greed, hardness, that she could not say at what point she'd begun to lose it. Even now she had no consciousness of a moral regeneration (if there were such a thing). She had changed, that was all—and many things had contributed.

What about the Cheyenne captivity she had schemed so tirelessly to escape? Really, aside from her being a prisoner—and other things—the interlude had been far from unpleasant. In fact she had taken to the life as a duck did to water. She had tanned like an Indian; she had thrived on the Cheyennes' Spartan life and rough fare. A girlhood spent in cramped and swarming cities had never permitted her more than a brushing acquaintance with sunlight and nature—things to which she now woke each day with a child's eager anticipation.

Cresta Marybelle Lee—an Army wife? Living out her youth walking a diplomatic tightrope of rigid observances in order to further her husband's career? Spending her matronly years pouring tea and making small talk with generals' fat wives? *Cresta Lee?*—the go-to-hell girl of all time?

What in God's name could she have been *thinking* of?

She laid her plate aside and got slowly to her feet, wiping her hands on her stag pants. Looking at McNair now, she did have a painful moment.

"I guess I'm a fool, Johnny. It should be you. Really. You're the kindest, most thoughtful—"

"Please." McNair fashioned a faint twisted grin. "You've never greased the axle before. Don't now. That's like rubbing it in. I know you don't mean to, but it. is."

"Then I don't know what to say, Johnny."

"I do. Skedaddle."

She went back to the wagon. Swinging up across the tailboard, she found that Honus was trying to pull himself up to a sitting position.

"For God's sake, Buster! Why?"

Honus slumped flat again, eying her almost balefully. His face was pale and sweat-sheened. "Just trying to see if I could sit up. And it's no concern of yours."

"Well, you found out." She yanked the blanket up to his chest again. "And it's damned *well* my concern if you're going to spend your life wrecking your health with damnfool stunts."

"That's right," he muttered. "My life. Why don't you tend to your own?"

"Well, I am. Sort of." She pulled herself up beside him, folded her legs beneath her, and made herself comfortable. Then began to lean toward him, softening her voice. "Yours. Mine. Ours, I mean. What do you think of that?"

He blinked cautiously. "Well, I, uh, I don't know. Er—I mean, do you mean—"

"Oh, for God's sake!" said Cresta Lee. She grabbed him by the ears and leaned all the way down. "*This* is what I mean. . . ."

The Scars of Dracula

ANGUS HALL

The Mark of the Fang

A moment of passion, an angry father, a quick escape on a runaway coach . . . and Paul found himself alone at dead of night on the open road.

An untended black coach provided refuge for a night of dreamless sleep. But the next morning the coach was no longer untended or on the open road.

It stood in the courtyard of a gaunt and eerie castle.

The castle of Count Dracula.

Now a Hammer Film for Associated British Productions released through MGM-EMI Distributors Ltd.
Starring Christopher Lee, Jenny Hanley, Dennis Waterman, Patrick Troughton and Christopher Matthews.
Produced by Aida Young.
Directed by Roy Ward-Baker.

Cromwell

JOHN BUCHAN

"John Buchan has brought to his task invaluable qualities – familiar knowledge of military affairs; shrewd understanding of men and their motives, both individually and in mass; imaginative insight into the issues and personalities of the time, irrespective of party."
Professor G. M. Trevelyan

John Buchan's superb account of one of the most turbulent periods in the history of Britain is now a Columbia film starring Richard Harris as Cromwell and Sir Alec Guinness as Charles I.

'NAKED CAME THE STRANGER'

is a dirty book.
One of the funniest, dirtiest
books of all time.

It's the story of Gillian Blake. And half
the male population of a chic
New York suburb.

Her appetite is insatiable. And she caters
for all tastes.

From zonked out hippies to a randy rabbi.
From a pornographer who wishes he
could practise what he preaches, to a
rather pretty young man who prefers not
to think about the war between the sexes.

'Naked Came The Stranger' was written
by Penelope Ashe. Penelope Ashe is the
pen name of thirteen randy Madison
Avenue ad-agency copywriters who set out
to write a funny dirty book.

They succeeded.

If you buy it, please don't leave it around
for kids, genteel maiden ladies, or people
with weak hearts to get hold of.

'NAKED CAME THE STRANGER'.
Penelope Ashe
25p

BOOKSHELF SPECIAL!

ONLY 132½p (26s 6d) Plus 24p (4s 9d) postage and packing

This three-shelf bookshelf is specially designed to fit your paperbacks. There's room for up to 120 standard size paperbacks. Each shelf has its own adjustable bookend to hold the books snugly in place.

It's handsome! It's made of very strong, very lightweight metal. The shelves are beautifully finished in matt white, yellow and red; sides and bookends in gunmetal grey.

It fits anywhere! Height 21″, width 19″, depth 4½″ (approx). You can fix it at floor level or eye level, above a bunk or beside a divan. It's easy to assemble: full instructions are enclosed.

You save almost the price of a fat new paperback! Order here and now on the coupon—and this bookshelf costs you only 132½pp (26s 6d) plus 24p (4s 9d) postage and packing. 156½p (31s 3d) altogether. This represents a saving of 34½p (7s) on the manufacturer's recommended price 191p (38s 3d) for a similar shelf in the shops.

Please fill in both parts of the coupon and send it with cheque or postal order, made payable to Sphere Bookshelf Offer to:
**Sphere Bookshelf Offer,
Orient House, Granby Row,
Manchester M1 7AU**
This offer is open only to readers in Gt Britain and N. Ireland. Closing date June 30th 1972.

Allow 21 days for delivery.

Sphere Bookshelf Offer (coupon)		
I enclose cheque/P.O. value	for	bookshelves
Name	Name	
Address	Address	
Town	Town	
County	County	

All Sphere Books are available at your bookshop or newsagent, or can be ordered from the following address:

Sphere Books, Cash Sales Department,
P.O. Box 11, Falmouth, Cornwall.

Please send cheque or postal order (no currency), and allow 5p per book to cover the cost of postage and packing in U.K., 7p per copy overseas.